Something Borrowed

Something Borrowed

edited by
JENNA JAMESON
with
M. CATHERINE OLIVERSMITH

SOUNDS PUBLISHING™

Savannah, Georgia

Text copyright © 2008 Sounds Publishing, Inc.

Published by Sounds Publishing, Inc.
     7400 Abercorn Street, Suite 705–300
     Savannah, GA 31406
     www.soundspublishing.com
     e-mail: info@soundspublishing.com

Library of Congress Control Number: 2008921057

ISBN-10: 0-9799872-0-2
ISBN-13: 978-0-9799872-0-5

First printing: May 2008

Printed and manufactured in the United States of America

10 9 8 7 6 5 4 3 2 1

For additional information on JennaTales, Erotica for the Woman on Top or to download audio erotica visit www.jennatales.com.

Distributed by Kensington Publishing Corp.

Submit Wholesale Orders to:
Kensington Publishing Corp.
C/O Penguin Group (USA) Inc.
Attention: Order Processing
405 Murray Hill Parkway
East Rutherford, NJ 07073-2316
Phone: 1-800-526-0275
Fax: 1-800-227-9604

*This second collection of amazing **JennaTales, Erotica for the woman on top,** is dedicated to everyone who believes in making possible the impossible. The stories are for people who set outrageous goals for their lives and who live outside the box, recognizing there is no path.*

Contents

Editor's Note

The response to *Something Blue,* the first book in the **Jenna-Tales,** *Erotica for the woman on top* anthology series has been so amazingly positive, proving the point that women want fun, sexy, wildly creative erotica that reflects their wide variety. Well, then, hang on to your hats, charge up your batteries (wink, wink), and find yourself a little bit of "me" time because we've done it again with *Something Borrowed.*

In *Something Blue,* we challenged readers with a new, quirky, sexy series, **JennaTales,** seeking to create something that would make you throw out your tired old-school erotica. I am happy to say *Something Blue* was right on the money. OW! I think I sprained my shoulder patting myself on the back.

But it isn't me, really, that did it. As editor, I have the great luck to work with fabulous authors who are inspired, wildly depraved, uninhibited, and prolific. I also have the amazing good fortune to work with Jenna Jameson, our muse for **JennaTales,** and she absolutely does review and approve every story herself. She's very involved, making suggestions and sharing her own ideas because these books really are her books, from cover to cover and every explicit, sexy, wonderful page between.

It definitely is a team effort to put together what we think of as the best mix of short stories that portray strong women who live full, liberated, sexually adventurous lives. Women just like our fans.

Just like *Something Blue, Something Borrowed* includes lots of entertaining tips and ideas for implementing positions, dealing with relationships, trying on a role, or tying up a friend and lover. We want you to have fun, to experiment, to let your wild side shine, and we want you to do it safely and with confidence you'll do it right. And, again, notes and quotes are included. You told us you loved them, so we made sure to have them here, because we want you to be happy. We're not unlike your mother that way.

I also wanted to shout out props to Mike Ruiz, the official photographer for the **JennaTales** series. He is a seriously talented artist with incredible vision. His work captures all that is alluring, sexy, tempting, and strong about Jenna and we are so fortunate to have his fantabulous portraits grace our covers. We think the books are worth the price just for the cover art. Think of it as buying a beautiful picture and getting hours of hot, wild, sexy entertainment as a bonus!

If you haven't yet, be sure to check out our audio erotica at www.JennaTales.com. Let us whisper sexy, hot stories in your ear while you relax for some hands-free pleasure. You can download them for instant gratification and there's a free story available to whet your appetite.

As always, enjoy, enjoy, enjoy!

—M. Catherine OliverSmith

Another good reason to wear a skirt to a party . . . or at least for the ride home.

Vanilla with Chocolate

Sally's house was set in the center of a suburban neighborhood with cookie-cutter houses, cul-de-sacs, and a child's bike in each driveway. It was a mecca of soccer moms and minivans, edged lawns, Sunday barbeques, and car pools. Todd, already breaking a sweat and feeling nauseous at the prospect of the evening to come pulled into one of the few available spaces along the curb and sat staring out the windshield.

"Well," he said in a monotone. "This is the place."

Poor Todd. He just hates parties. We're like apples and oranges (or apples and cement blocks) when it comes to people and parties. Todd and I have been married for over three years and he is a wonderful guy, just not very gregarious.

"You sure you want to go in there, Bev?" The engine was still running and I swear he gunned it.

"Of course I want to go in. I promised Sally that we'd come. I know you hate parties, but we're going to this one, damn it."

"But this isn't just any party, Bev. She's selling sex toys!"

"Don't be a prude, Todd. It'll be fun. You'll see."

Todd stuck his lower lip out, crossed his arms across his chest, and hunkered down in the seat looking not unlike Tommy Scotto, the most awful, intractable third grader I'd ever run up against.

"Okay then. Why don't you wait here, in the car," I suggested. "I'll only be a couple hours. Having wine and talking about sex with other people." He got the hint.

Walking up to the house, he dragged his feet, scuffing the toes of the nice leather loafers I'd bought him just a week ago. I swear there are times that I feel like I married my job, being an elementary teacher at school and home.

Sally threw the door wide, inviting us in with a big smile and a kiss on my cheek and wink to Todd. He almost did an about-face, but I had his arm in an iron grip, so he nodded and mumbled something closely resembling a greeting at Sally's shoes before peering nervously around the corner into the living room, where a dozen couples were already chatting amiably over wine and crackers.

It was an eclectic group. I wore a white summer cotton skirt, flip-flops, and a tiny ice-blue tank. Others were in jeans or shorts, while there were a few in business skirts or suits. I noticed that the couples were mostly sticking together, but occasionally the women would start talking more candidly, sharing intimacies the way only women who've just met over a glass of wine can, while the guys generally tried to blend into the background, which was nearly impossible since Sally's taste lent itself to a blend of wild safari and sunshine yellow and none of them appeared to be wearing bright yellow, monkey-covered shirts. Of course, if one of them had, I probably wouldn't have been able to see him as that would have been the perfect camouflage in Sally's living room. That's Sally all over. Great girl, lousy sense of color.

Sally came by with a tray of veggies and dip, trailed by an attractive brunette about my age in a crisp, off-white tailored suit.

"Bev, have a cucumber and meet Heather. Heather's my friend from the firm I was telling you about." Heather is a "dildo pusher on the side" is what Sally had actually said a week and a half ago when, over a carafe of sangria and shared, illicit cigarettes, she finally got up the guts to invite us to this shindig.

"I've heard such amazing things about you." I smiled at Sally then Heather, trying to keep a straight face as visions of a cucumber vibrator suddenly flashed across my imagination. I bit into the cuke in my hand, setting my teeth to keep from laughing hysterically, and managed rather well to appear sane. Sally whisked Heather away, kicking me in the shin as she went. I guess I wasn't as cool as I'd thought. Then I almost choked to death from laughing because I realized I wasn't as cool as a "cucumber." I had to get some water and stop on the wine or I'd be intolerable. Todd had been gone for so long, I thought he'd left me there. Just as we were all sitting down, he slunk back into the room. I glared and he shrugged. I wanted to ask where he'd been, but Heather was already introducing herself, so I'd just have to let it go.

"I was trying not to get sick in the bathroom," Todd hissed to me, knowing that I was stewing and frustrated that he'd disappeared on me.

"Todd . . . ler." I hissed back. "Way too much time with third graders" will be my epitaph if I don't get a handle on myself.

I'll admit, however, that I was a bit embarrassed at first when Heather started talking about my vulva. Not mine, per se, but *the* vulva, which made me think of mine, which embarrassed me. I got over it, though. I realized that everyone was feeling about the same as me. Also, I had grabbed another glass of wine despite my excellent intentions and that was definitely helping as well. Heather knew what she was saying and eventually I think we all felt comfortable, except for Todd.

Heather started the evening by putting a CD in the player. It had some nice music, but then a voice started. Turns out that it was a sample of a series of CDs Heather sells. It was a short story, she told us. People were still murmuring and chatting a little when suddenly the story started talking about her heavy breasts and his bobbing cock. That got everyone's attention. Turns out the short stories were erotic. Heather told us they were great for getting in the mood. It was hard to do in the middle of the party, but I could totally see what she was talking about. Just the bit I was listening to was pretty steamy, and I knew it would get downright boiling hot as I imagined relaxing in the tub, listening, with a glass of wine.

"We've got to get one of those." I hissed at Todd.

"Well, the Sugar series sounds sweet." He joked, badly.

"How about a little Spank!" I replied. I wasn't joking.

Heather then began showing her products. There were oils with sparkles and flavored oils and oils that heated up on contact. The room relaxed a lot once she handed around small samples. She encouraged couples to rub the oils on one another and most did, almost exclusively on the hands, although one imaginative guy did smear some on his wife's neck and then licked it off. People were definitely getting more into the party.

"Smell this, Todd," I thrust a bottle under his nose.

"Almond." He guessed correctly. "I don't know, Bev. Smells like you should cook with it, not rub it anywhere."

Heather went on to exhibit a variety of other sexy items including sheer panties, female-directed adult movies, and orgasm-enhancing lotion. She handed out little samples of that, too. I put a little on the back of my hand and it grew warm.

"Oooh, that tingles!" I heard a giggle from the corner and saw that one woman had reached under her top and put it on her nipple.

Heather also pulled up an impressive array of condoms. Flavored, ribbed, rippled, extra large . . . She gave a free 12-pack to the person who got the most answers right on her sex quiz. To Todd's chagrin, I won.

Finally, Heather pulled out the big guns. She had the rubber-ducky vibrator for tub-time fun, the rabbit, remote-control vibrating panties, and so many other things I hadn't even dreamed existed.

She also had a huge array of dildos. Twisty, curvy, shiny cocks in every imaginable color, some in the shape of animals, others with humorous faces. I was mesmerized.

Todd, noticing the gleam in my eyes, asked, "Have you ever used one of those?"

"Oh, no," I lied. Well, it wasn't a total lie. I hadn't used any of the ones she was showing.

"Have you?" I asked, not bothering to whisper. Todd blushed crimson.

"You want the *purple* one," he said loudly to get even.

"Purple? Please." I wasn't going to be bested.

"Well, what color, then?" He thought he had trumped me because he sure didn't expect me to have an answer.

There was one vibrating, rotating cock that had immediately caught my eye. It was nine inches long, and batteries were included! What a deal.

"The Chocolate Thunder." I won. Todd was shocked into silence.

"But, but . . ." he stuttered. "It's so long." I almost made a mean-spirited comment, but it would be a lie. Todd's no slouch in that department.

Heather began to thank everyone for showing up, and offered to take orders in one of the spare bedrooms.

I was the first in line. Todd had, somehow, skipped out to the car. Heather explained that she didn't have every item on hand. Luckily for me, she had Chocolate Thunder. I also picked up one of each of the CDs. My sister would love the Sugar ones. Saying good-bye to Sally, I headed for the car. I barely had my seatbelt buckled when Todd tore out of there like demons from hell were behind us. I had to remind him it was a family neighborhood to get him to slow it down a bit.

"Did you order it?" Todd asked while I slid all over the passenger's seat as he took a fifteen-mile-an-hour curve at thirty.

Once we were back on the straight and narrow and he'd finally eased up a bit on the gas, I tugged the vibrator out of the bag. "Mmmmm . . ." I hummed happily. "She had it in stock." I laughed at his wide-open mouth.

Opening the package and gently pulling the long rubbery piece out, I accidentally turned it on, causing it to whir and shake.

"You aren't going to use that thing now?" Todd was ready to panic.

"Why not? It's mine. I bought it." I hadn't planned to, but what a great idea, I thought.

"You haven't even cleaned it yet," he challenged.

"It was in a box, for God's sake, Todd. But if it makes you feel better . . ." I pulled out the free condom pack I'd won. Taking a vanilla flavored condom, I rolled it onto my now stilled dildo. I stopped every inch or so, enjoying the feel of the staff.

Todd drove carefully, but tried to keep at least one eye on what I was doing.

Once I'd gotten the condom on, I started licking it, just beneath the head. It tasted just like vanilla. Well it tasted just like vanilla in a rubber cone, but still a close enough approximation.

"What are you doing?" Todd asked. As though he couldn't tell.

I pushed the cock into my mouth, just a little at first then I fed it deeper, until its head tapped my throat. I hummed, simulating its vibrations. Hiking up my skirt, I took the wet dildo from my mouth and held it against my thigh, enjoying the blackness of it against my creamy leg. I pushed my panties to the side and slipped the head in me. I turned it on. WOW! It vibrated and shook in me, turning me to jelly.

"Bev!" Todd almost yelled. I was way too busy and too hot to reply. I didn't care about the busy highway either. I began to orgasm before the vibrator was halfway into me. My back arched. My shoulders shuddered. My hips bucked and my heels kicked. My left hand reached out and grabbed on to Todd's arm as my moans mixed with the horn blasts of a trucker.

When we got home, Todd had gotten over his shock. After carrying me up to bed and ravishing me for several good hours, he was just starting to fall asleep when I leaned over for one final surprise.

"Todd, I start training next week."

"Training" he mumbled.

"Yep, Heather's training me to present at parties." I snuggled down to sleep as Todd's eyes shot wide.

C. J. Stone

JennaTip #1: Vibrators

Not to discount the multitudes of women who orgasm through G-spot stimulation or nipple stimulation or by thinking about it just because they can, the reality is that most women do require direct clitoral stimulation to achieve orgasm. While a nice firm and wet tongue or talented finger can do the job very nicely, the consistent and powerful vibration of a personal toy delivers unlike anything else.

If you are not completely familiar with using a vibrator, stop reading and go buy one right now and then come back with a fresh supply of batteries (unless you opt for the plug-in variety) and pick the book back up. The plug-in vibrators can be great because they are quieter, by and large, but you are tethered to an outlet; then again, you don't run out of juice late at night and have to steal batteries from the TV remote. There are new rechargeable vibrators out there and also ergonomic ones that keep you from suffering from wrist and hand cramps. You certainly don't want to try to figure out a way to explain to your friends and coworkers how you got carpal tunnel syndrome when you don't use a keyboard.

Once you have the vibrator you want, the following is a guide for how to enjoy yourself.

1. ***Setting the mood.*** Do not try out your new toy without allowing yourself some uninterrupted time. For example, trying out a vibrator ten minutes before the kids are due home from school is probably not the best planning unless you find working under a deadline really titillating. Instead plan out a good block of time, shower or have a nice hot bath first, pamper yourself, use oils and lotions to moisturize your skin, listen to some music, or read some hot erotica (you know where you can find some).

2. ***Don't just go gung-ho for the clit.*** Press the vibrator against your breast, your thigh, your outer labia, and your nipples. Try it anywhere. It is a great way to get to know your body.

3. ***Go gung-ho for your clit.*** Once you are sufficiently aroused (read *wet*) move the vibrator down to your clit and test your reaction. Some women are unable to put the vibrator directly against the clit and have to put it at the head of the mons or cover it with their labia because it is too intense. Go ahead and move it around, press it harder, then softer, use the side, the tip, have it rest along your entire vulva, roll it around. Experiment and have fun.

4. ***Go for the combo.*** Want vaginal penetration with vibration? Use two vibrators, a vibrator and dildo, a vibrator and your finger or someone else's finger, use a vibrator and a penis, or use a dual-action vibe that has a penetrating piece and a little added stimulator for the clit. There are any number of possible and yummy combinations.

In case you have any qualms about introducing a vibrator into your repertoire, keep the following in mind. There is nothing wrong with using a vibrator. Do you use a hair dryer for your hair? It'll dry on its own, won't it? Do you have an electric blender? You could use a spoon, right? So how is it different to use a vibrator to stimulate your clitoris or G-spot? It isn't. If your husband/lover/partner has any problems with your using it, ask him to toss out his electric razor, power drill, and any adult videos or magazines he uses to jack off. Down with hypocrisy!

I never thought of the runway as phallic. Now that I think about it, that's it exactly. It makes sense. Mostly it's women walking the runway and I can just see a man designing it so that women are walking up and down a cock. Makes me want to dig out a pair of spike heels.

Moonlighting

It was called Buff Bubba's Ranch, which didn't leave much doubt about how tacky the place would be. It was large, airplane-hangar large, with just one big room and a smattering of chairs and tables. The windows were high. Obviously and unfortunately they were too high to clean. And the brown carpet, what was left of it, smelled like perfume and gin.

There must have been over a hundred women in the place: young, giggly women; old, prim women; women of every shape and age and status.

Straight ahead of me was the stage. It wasn't nearly as large as I'd imagined. Only two steps wide, and a few car lengths long. I suppose it was meant to be phallic. On it was a man wearing just a bikini bottom. The black skin of his shaved body glistened in response to the lights as he danced around the arena.

I moved to the bar, which was a long, twisting piece of wood and brass, manned by a few young men in thongs.

"What'll you have?" the bartender asked.

"Cosmo. Please."

"Right up." He smiled, too long, before he turned around and bent down, straight legged, to a bottom shelf, searching for what I hoped would be a clean martini glass. His thong covered up less of his butt than a shadow would have and his cheeks wiggled at me as he shuffled things around.

"That's my favorite drink, too." A woman eased up beside me, set her near-full glass on the bar, and joined in my view. The bartender found what he needed, entirely too soon for her, based on her disgusted sigh as he turned back around to face us, then he was off for some crushed ice and vodka.

"I'm Brenda," she said. She was a brunette, pretty, well tanned. I didn't know if this was normal, this being my first trip to a strip club. I would have thought people wouldn't talk to one another, but I guess that's really more a guy thing than a woman thing. Women will talk to each other anywhere.

"Lisa," I said, and we daintily shook hands.

"Been here before? Are you alone?"

"First time. Just me." I was embarrassed admitting it. What kind of woman was I to be at a strip club alone? I felt like I just admitted to drinking bourbon with my cornflakes.

"I'm alone, too. My friends are too chicken to come here. But I love it. Try to come at least once a week, if not more. How about sitting together? My table is right by the stage. Best view in the house."

I nodded okay, waited for my drink, then followed Brenda through the place. I don't think I'd been in a crowd of so many women since high school gym class. I hoped she wasn't hitting on me, but I chastised myself for assuming I was that attractive and ignoring the illogic of her coming to see men strip every week if she preferred women. Maybe she was bi. I decided to shut myself up and took a sip of my drink.

She was right about where her seat was. It was at the very tip of the stage, so close that I could see footprints on the lacquered runway. I was at the head of the wooden cock.

"The newer guy is next. He's only been here a couple weeks, but he's damn hot." Brenda sucked on her drink.

It was just after nine o'clock. This "newer guy" about to

come out was David. My David. The guy I'd lived with for three years.

It would appear that David had been laid off from his programming job three weeks ago, not that he had told me. Our arrangement was that we shared equally in expenses and chores. I cooked and he did the dishes. I did the laundry and he vacuumed. And, as I mentioned, we shared equally in the expenses, splitting the bills fifty-fifty. Apparently, he lost his job and instead of telling me all about it as he should have done, he had tried to quickly find another one, been unsuccessful in the short term, and had started moonlighting as a male stripper at this hellhole of a barn. That is, he failed to share this tidbit of information with me until last night, when he admitted that, rather than working late nights in the office, he'd been stripping at Buff Bubba's Ranch.

I should have known something was up when he bought me the new earrings with diamonds and sapphires out of the blue. Or when he one day presented me with La Perla lingerie. Bras that cost upward of $500 are not generally in our budget. Then there were the lunches. Every Thursday he was taking me out to lunch, paying for the whole tab, and choosing really nice places.

But I was not paying enough attention to these details, happy in my ignorance. I don't know what made him finally come clean, but he did, and now here I was to see for myself just what my David had been doing to make what was apparently three times what he made as a programmer.

David peeked out of the curtain, like his head was testing unfamiliar water. Brenda jumped up and screamed when she saw him. Others joined her, sounding like groupies. He slipped out from behind the tacky silver and black shiny material that pretended to be a curtain wearing a leather biker outfit. Well, a Village People kind of leather biker outfit, with lots of silver and tassels.

The pants stuck to him like a wet paper towel and the jacket, zipped down to mid-chest, flowered into a wide collar that embraced his face.

David's an attractive man with his dark brown hair, green eyes, and a refined face that generally is wreathed by a relaxed smile. He's trim, muscled, but not so much that his body lacks a certain fluidity. I didn't think he saw me, and I slunk back into my chair, trying to blend into the crowd.

The music, a rock beat with a dash of salsa to it, turned louder, and David stepped directly into a dance. My jaw dropped when he turned away from me and I saw that the leather pants were cut out in the back. There. A hundred chicks just saw my David's fine ass. And damn, did they like it. Wolf whistles almost drowned out the music.

But David kept his beat. Kicking around. Slamming his behind into an invisible wall. He was sweating in less than a minute. From the bottom strands of his hair, wet, small beads dripped to his nearly hairless chest. Soon, the jacket was off and skidding backstage. Next the pants, which he pulled off in front of him with a snap, went flying up over his head.

The girls went wild and, I'll admit, David looked pretty damn hot on that stage, bouncing around in nothing but a thin leather thong. Whenever he neared the edge of the deck, and he did so often, a flurry of women would race over to him and jam cash into the thong's thin straps. His waist was looking like a bushel of lettuce by the time he made it to the head of the stage, just a couple yards away from me.

Brenda, clasping a ten-dollar bill, reached up to him. He worked into her, swaying his hips until his leathered sac was within her reach. She stuffed the bill into his front, her hand lingering and then she did it.

All I can say is that she's lucky I hadn't gotten there a few drinks earlier, or I would have slapped her with a chair. She actually grabbed his package, cupping him in her palm. I was thinking she had better be a doctor and he had better turn and cough when I glared up at him and that's exactly when David saw me. Our eyes met for a moment as his face flushed red. He froze. I don't even think he realized that Brenda's hand was still on him as I left, racing for my car and driving home at breakneck speed.

It was only thirty minutes later when David arrived at our apartment. As he stepped into the dark living room, he saw me sitting on the couch. He was dressed in street clothes: black jeans, and a white button-up shirt. He looked upset as hell and attempted to stammer an explanation.

"Quiet," I said as I tossed a crumpled-up twenty by his feet before flicking on a reading light and flashing the beam directly into his face.

"Strip, David. Strip. Just for me."

David began to dance.

Ramo Kye

Once upon a time . . . my God, was someone following me around and taking notes? This girl is one in a million. She's a balls-to-the-wall chick looking for Mr. Right Now!

Girl Gone Wild

I'm really more reserved than this story sets me up to be, but once I've had a few drinks, and by a few, I mean four plus, I have this thing about being naked. Well, maybe not naked as in stripper naked, but naked as in peep show.

Sometimes, I just lean forward a little and let guys get a peek down my top, a little looky-loo at my creamy, milky, swaying breasts. Other times, I pull up my shirt for a quick flash. It depends, I think, on whether I am in a bar or restaurant or in a dance club or outside or in a moving vehicle. The flash is totally a moving-vehicle kind of stunt, while the let-them-look-down-the-top is more of a lean-on-the-table move.

Totally Girls Gone Wild, I know, but I've been doing this for years and never once did I end up on video. Well, not on any video that I know about. I guess through the years I was limiting my exhibitionism to normal bars in normal towns and not at crazy, drunken spring break fests.

As far as I am concerned, and that's really the bar I aim to hit, it doesn't count as stripper naked if I'm skinny-dipping. At least that's how I look at it. If the weather is warm and there is a body of water anywhere around, I am likely to strip down for a swim. I may then climb out of the water and lie around naked, but I'm not pole dancing, I'm relaxing.

So, as this particular story goes, I saw this really hot guy, and I checked him out before my happy two hours of drinks, so I wasn't beer-goggling (or Appletini-goggling either) and knew

15

he started out hot and was still hot, and he was sitting across a trendy upscale little martini bar from me.

I was sitting at a bar table, one of the tall ones with the tall chairs, and he was in a booth, so his eyes were about level with my crotch, which gave me the idea. I'd been making some eye contact now and again, smiling, glancing, pushing my auburn hair behind my ears, just the sort of thing that generally worked in these situations. I couldn't flash the breasts because of the difference in height, what with me being too high and whatnot. Also, the boob flash is more for shock than as a pick-up. And I was definitely trying for a pick-up. In addition, I think I may have been tossed out on my shapely ass if I really flashed someone in this bar, what with the velvet ropes and "having to know someone or blow someone just to get in" reputation it had.

I'd done the whole *Basic Instinct* cross-and-uncross my legs, giving him a flash of panty. He was definitely looking, but I wasn't getting any buying signals. Could I get more obvious? Of course I could.

I stood, thrusting the bottom of my clingy top into the waistband of my skirt. My top hugged my ample tits nicely as I sashayed past him, thrusting my luscious breasts out and swaying my hips side to side, pausing at the corner of the bar before, with one last lingering look, I walked down the hallway to get in the long-ass line for the women's room.

Well, I got his attention and the attention of about half the guys in the bar. But he still wasn't getting up and making his way over to me. I mean, seriously, I'm making an effort here and all I wanted was for him to walk about fifteen paces to me, buy me a drink, then take me to my place, where I'd climb up on top of him and fuck him cross-eyed. A girl does want some of that old-time romance, after all.

Therefore, I realized it was time for drastic action. In the bathroom, I removed my panties and clenched them in my hand. On my way back from the bathroom, I stopped right at his table, as though to adjust the strap of my little fuck-me pumps, and then upon straightening back up with a very nice "bend and snap" move straight from *Legally Blonde,* placed my balled-up undies on the table right next to his glass. I looked him right in his dark, sexy eyes, licked my lips, and said, loud and clear:

"Oops. I appear to have lost my panties. Should someone hot and sexy with dark hair and a chiseled jaw happen to locate them, I'll be out in the parking lot, leaning provocatively up against my car, the blue BMW convertible."

Before he could react at all, I had picked up my purse, tossed money on the table to cover my bill and a tip, and was out the door.

I was leaning against the trunk of my car when he came up to me.

"I believe these belong to you." He said it so seriously I wondered if I had made a mistake. Then he put both hands on either side of my hips and leaned in hard, pressing himself between my legs, forcing them apart and making my skirt ride up my thighs.

Smiling I said, "Why, yes, those do look like mine. I do believe I may have misplaced them in the bar. I can't be sure, however, in this light."

"Well, what do you suggest?" He joked back.

I was enjoying this banter, this foreplay we had going.

"I imagine that if those truly were mine, they'd have my signature scent."

Well, that made his eyes pop out a bit. Then he lifted the wet panties up to his nose, buried his face in them, and really inhaled. I was getting really hot about this time. Okay. I was already hot and horny. I was about melting by this time.

"Sweet and creamy. Good combination," he said after lowering the panties from his face. Then he lifted me up by my hips, putting me fully onto the trunk of my car, slid my skirt all the way up, pushed my thighs even farther apart, and buried his head right in my pussy. He sniffed, tasted, licked, sucked, and nearly caused me to die right there.

When he came up for air, he had a big, wet smile on his face.

"Yep. These must be yours. Same scent. Same taste."

I had planned on taking him back to my place for a wham, bam, and thank-you-very-much-and-don't-let-the-door-hit-you-on-the-ass fuck, but I couldn't wait, and I guess neither could he.

He unzipped his pants, pulled out the largest, hardest, beast of a cock I'd seen in quite some time, particularly in a parking lot. Once he'd freed the animal, he pulled me down to the edge of the car and rammed that lovely one-eyed snake up into me, massaging my breast with one hand while the other steadied me in place and his tongue danced along my neck and into my mouth.

God, he was great. I came almost immediately. After a little bit, he turned me around, bent me over the car, and went at me from behind. I think I scratched up the paint on the trunk with my rings and bracelets as I tried to hang on for dear life. I didn't really care then, and don't really care now. I'm surprised there isn't a permanent dent from my body the way it was slammed and pressed into that car.

I came again. And again.

Finally, he pulled out and turned me back around. I knew exactly what he wanted and my mouth was watering as I dropped to my knees. I got gravel embedded in my kneecaps, but I didn't care. I wrapped my wet swollen lips around that dripping hard cock of his and sucked him, bobbing up and down, tonguing the tip and fondling his balls until I knew he was going to totally lose it. He came in big spurts and I loved every last bit.

I straightened up. Thanked him for finding and returning my favorite panties. He said, "I think I have to hold on to these. You don't seem to be very responsible and they are much too precious to chance losing again."

He pocketed them and strolled away back into the bar.

Francis Underwood

JennaTip #2: That Girl

Are you "That Girl"? The one that can actually go to a cool bar by herself, have a couple drinks, check out the catalog of available men, pick out the lucky winner of the night, make your move, have great, orgasmic, no-commitments sex, and say a cheerful good-bye, neither hoping to see him again or caring much if you do?

Then you are one in a million!

If you are that kind of woman, then have fun, be wild, and be crazy. Just, please, be careful. You can have lots of fun, just don't put yourself in unsafe situations. First, don't have unprotected sex with strangers. Always use a condom and your common sense. Worry less about whether it will spoil the mood and more about how getting an STD (sexually transmitted disease) can very well spoil your life. Use a latex condom, not lambskin, as the lambskin is not as safe. Make sure your condom is not expired. They do have expiration dates. Don't store it in heat or direct sunlight. Use one that has a spermicidal lubricant. You can go ahead and use other lubes, get glow-in-the-dark or funky colors, use ones that have ridges or bumps or ticklers for all I care. Just be certain to use one. Sorry if this isn't the sexiest advice you've ever gotten, but a clean and healthy body is much sexier than the alternative.

Now, as to having wild-and-crazy sex in public, you do want to be careful in other ways. Be sure that you don't attract the attention of the wrong element, which includes security and the police who may arrest you, but also means you don't want some drunk (or sober) dumb asshole who thinks because you are having amazing consensual sex in public you're willing to have sex with him or his stupid shithead friends. Remember, not all guys are good guys.

Now, how to have great outdoor sex: Have him lift your thigh up to his hip and hold it there with his arm; grab your ass with his other hand. You will have one foot still on the ground and can hold on to him around his neck or put your arms back and your hands on the hood or trunk of your car. He will be providing support while thrusting into you as you both are standing to avoid dents and scratches in the car from your jewelry.

For ways to have sex in your car, see the Sex in Cars tip later in the book. If you are doing this in the rain, be sure it isn't a lightning storm. If there is no chance of being electrocuted (not exactly the sort of tingling sensation you should be seeking), sex outside in the rain can be so incredible. It's like being in the shower, but for some reason your skin will be more sensitive to the rain, probably just from being out in the open as opposed to being behind a curtain or shower door. Mostly, have fun and feel good.

I like a little give and take, though some days I'm all for
taking while someone else is doing the giving. A favorite
quote of mine is: "I don't want the world, I just want your
half." ("Ana Ng"—They Might Be Giants). Read the
story and you'll understand the quote.

Winner Takes Half

At six feet, one-half inches in my bare feet, I'm a tall, lithe force to be reckoned with and, except for my rather impressive breasts, I'm triathlete thin with long legs that do go all the way up, toned arms, and a mane of red hair I streak with gold for even greater impact. I'm called "Tigress."

Now, I know you're thinking with that description I must be a female wrestler or in the circus. The truth is much more exotic, at least it is to me.

By the time I was nineteen, I'd made my first million. Since then, I've focused on devouring small companies, sucking the marrow from the bones, and spitting out the slivers when I'm done.

The same can be said for my sex life. I fuck small men, sucking out their marrow and spitting the slivers out when I'm done. I don't mean short men or skinny men when I say small. It's just that most men are small to me: in mind, in vision, in bed. I used to fuck my personal trainer, but he couldn't keep up, couldn't keep anything up.

I ate men up like peanuts, an unsatisfying snack, but enough to keep the hunger at bay, until a real meal. The problem was I never found a real meal of a man to sink my teeth into, so I was constantly ravenous.

I'd recently instructed my people to buy Alpha Nonferrous

Metal, Inc., through a company I owned 51 percent of, Manx Properties. When they brought me the paperwork I was pleased, at first. The price was far less than I'd been willing to pay. Then I got to a clause on page seventeen. It gave the seller of ANFM, Randolph Stone, an option to buy three hundred shares of Manx Properties. If he exercised that option, I'd lose control of Manx. I'd still be the largest shareholder, but I wouldn't hold the majority.

I called my people. They assured me that they'd put out an order to buy enough additional shares in Manx to cover the three hundred, plus some.

That seemed fine, until I was called the next day. There were no shares in Manx available. Three small companies had bought up the 49 percent I didn't own—and all three were controlled by Randolph Stone. With the ANFM deal, he had control. He had the outstanding 49 percent, plus three hundred of my shares.

The bastard!

He'd used Manx's purchase of ANFM to gain control of Manx and keep control of his own company. I admired the slick way he moved, but I wouldn't let him win. I got my research people on it, finding out everything they could about Mr. Stone, from the color of his mother's eyes to where he bought his socks.

Meanwhile, I phoned him and arranged a lunch. I told him I'd send a car. He said he'd rather drive himself. I insisted. He gave in. That was a good start. Round One to me.

I'd insisted because of my driver. Silvia is a slender, beautiful blonde. She's useful for distracting men when I need them distracted, as well as for driving.

To the lunch, I wore a single-breasted business suit with nothing under my jacket. When we shook hands, his eyes were level with mine, but I was wearing four-inch heels and he wasn't. He also kept eye contact. He had a deep chest and broad shoulders, but he moved with elegant grace. Sexy and very disciplined. Either that or gay, and my people assured me he was straight as a highway in Oklahoma.

"Do your friends call you 'Randy'?" I asked, flirtatiously.

He gave me a flat, "No." Round two definitely to him.

I turned on the charm; reached across the table to touch his arm from time to time and kept working to get his eyes away from my face and onto my chest. Normally I'd be impressed with his ability to focus on the conversation, but I was trying to seduce my shares away from him. The bait was good, but the fish weren't biting one damn bit, at least not at first. By the time we had coffee, we'd at least progressed to "Randolph" and "Susan."

"That stock option," I said.

"Yes?"

"I'd like to buy it from you. Shall we say, twice market value?"

"I don't think so."

"Name your price," I offered.

"If ever I decide to sell it instead of exercising it, I'll call you first."

"Thanks." I paused. "I hear that you run." It was an understatement. He was obsessed with running.

"Yes, I do, some." He was playing nonchalant.

"Are you any good?"

He grinned. "I'll save time. You are making the attempt to maneuver me into a race, with the option as a prize. What are you putting up as your wager?"

"An equal number of my own shares."

"Interesting. I accept, but for a hundred shares, not the three."

"Scared of losing?" I taunted him.

"Prolonging an amusing game. Where? When? What distance?"

We met at six in the morning, at the reservoir. I had Silvia posed nicely against my Mercedes when he arrived. My shorts were brief and my racer-back red and black running shirt tight. He gave us both a long appreciative look.

"It's just over eight miles around," I told him.

"That's not my distance," he confessed, "but I'll try to cope."

I knew it wasn't his distance. I also knew he'd be up for the challenge.

Silvia fired a starter's pistol. I took off. When I couldn't hear him following, I glanced back. I was fifty feet ahead and he was just starting. Slow off the mark, Randolph!

He stayed fifty feet behind me until the last quarter-mile, when he overtook me with an easy, long, loping stride. I went flat out and finished no more than five feet behind him, but behind him.

"What's your distance?" I asked him when I caught my breath.

"The half-marathon. I try to get one in at least once a week."

They told me he was a runner and did distance, but I assumed my researchers meant either something shorter, which would have made him exhausted with eight miles, or a full marathon, which meant he would have had a hard time adjusting his stride to a quick enough pace.

Bastards! If he was used to thirteen miles, my eight was just a warm-up for him but not too short.

I offered, "Tennis? Three sets, two hundred shares?"

I had won singles at my club every year for forever.

"Racquetball?" he countered.

I'm not as good at it, but still my best game is incredibly hard to beat.

"Agreed!"

I pulled out all the stops. I always used everything in my arsenal when going after big game, and Randolph Stone was by far the largest trophy I'd set my sights on in years, if ever. I dressed to distract, with a loose, cropped top and skimpy volleyball shorts, demanding nothing of Randolph's imagination.

Racquetball is a vigorous game. The way I was dressed, I'd be flashing my breasts even if I tried not to, and I wasn't going to try not to. You have to focus on the ball, every fraction of a second. I was confident that with my tits bouncing before his eyes, he wouldn't be able to see that little ball bounce and ricochet.

First set, I beat him by five points. I offered, "Double the stakes?"

"Sure."

The next two sets he beat me by three and then eight points. I was limp and sagging. He was still bouncing on the balls of his feet. I can't recall ever hating a man so intensely.

"Darts?" he suggested with a grin "Chess? Backgammon? Arm wrestling?"

Okay, he had testosterone on his side, but there are some games where that can be a handicap. I intended to exploit his very maleness.

"Let me take you to dinner. Tomorrow night," I countered. "We can sort our business differences out in a civilized way." Those who know me will tell you that "civilized" is not in my vocabulary, particularly when I'm faced with losing. And I was losing not only these silly challenges, I was losing my company and my identity.

My offices take up the forty-seventh and forty-eighth floors of the tower. *The Last Tango* is a Spanish restaurant and club on the ground floor. The atmosphere is exotic and dangerous. I dressed with care. My gown was black knit silk jersey, very thin, very clinging. Its hem brushed the toes of my pumps. It had long sleeves and a high neck but was backless all the way down to my tailbone. It was impossible to wear anything under that dress, not that I tried. I wanted to distract Randolph Stone. I intended to keep his attention away from the subtle maneuvering I needed to do to gain back control. I wanted control of Manx again and I wanted control of him.

Randolph wore a tuxedo that fitted him as if it had been sewn together while he stood still for it. He didn't look surprised when I ordered a twenty-ounce bloody steak, seared and spiced on the outside. He had shark, with a side of jalapenos that he ate whole. If the meal was a competition in "machismo," which it was, I called it a tie.

Between courses, we danced. He couldn't hold me without putting his hand on my bare skin. The tango is danced body to body. His height and my heels put our hips right together, creating friction in all the right places.

No matter what you may think of me, I wasn't whoring to get back my business. I didn't grind against him or shamelessly throw myself at him. I simply used all my assets to put him in a good mood.

It worked. I was smugly satisfied with feeling his cock thicken inside his pants. By the third dance, his fingertips were lightly massaging my coccyx.

I pulled back and suggested, "Shall we continue this upstairs, in my office?"

"Continue what?"

My mouth said, "Our negotiations." The way I looked and leaned against him, pressing my hot sex against his hard crotch, suggested the negotiations were not necessarily about the shares.

I was prepared to fend him off if he tried to kiss me in the elevator, but he didn't. I was sure he wanted to, though.

I put dim art lights on in my office and crossed to my oversized rosewood desk. Perched on its edge, I told Randolph, "I think I have an offer you won't refuse."

"That's possible," he said, "but improbable."

Cocky as ever.

Undeterred, I continued, "I have a place on Maui, actually more of an estate than a 'place.' It's breathtakingly beautiful and very, very private. In exchange for my keeping control of Manx, I'm offering you a month in a tropical paradise, with a lovely and very wicked woman to keep you amused."

He took a step closer. His face darkened. "Let me get this straight," he said, with ice in his words. "Are you offering to prostitute yourself to me in exchange for a few lousy shares?"

"Of course not, you clod. I'm not available to you. You're not my type. I prefer powerful men."

His face darkened with the blood and anger that rushed to it.

"I'm offering you Silvia. My driver. I know you've noticed her and I thought she'd be about your speed."

Then, almost casually, I slapped him across the face.

"What was that for?" he demanded, shocked.

"For suggesting I am a whore."

"Never, ever, slap me again," his voice was low and growling.

"I don't expect I will have need to again." I was starting to circle him, like a tigress circles her prey.

"So, you're no whore. Then you must be some kind of pimp or madam. I should have known you'd be a whoremonger based on the way you've flaunted yourself before me." His sarcasm irked me, causing my fingers to twitch and my muscles to bunch.

I tried again to slap him, but Randolph caught my wrists this time and doubled them up behind my back. My knee drove up at his balls but bounced off a hard thigh. I was spun round, and pushed down over my desk.

I've trained in kung fu for years, but I wasn't a match for his size and strength. I knew I wouldn't be. He may have thought he had me where he wanted me, but I was actually the one in control now. We were playing my game and on my turf. At this, my expertise was unrivaled.

His hands were big enough and strong enough that he could pin my wrists together with just one. I kicked back at his shins but missed.

"You bastard," I repeated. "Unhand me immediately. I'll sue you. I'll have you arrested and charged with assault. Fuck you, Randolph Stone!"

"Is that how you thought you would get the shares back, you manipulative bitch?" He was afraid, I could tell, but that wasn't my ultimate plan. He released me and backed away.

"No, Randolph. I wasn't trying to rile you so you would manhandle me and I could sue, though it isn't such a bad idea." I was teasing at this point, but he was now unsteady and unsure, for the very first time.

"I apologize for grabbing you. I think I can argue self-defense. You are a powerful woman, trained in kung fu . . ." My sharp intake of breath interrupted him.

"Yes, I know about your kung fu. I had you researched as much as you tried to research me. What your people didn't, and couldn't, know was that I was feeding them just slightly inaccurate information. For example, I let it be known that I was a two-miler, not a half-marathoner."

I was duly impressed by how he'd been working behind the scenes from the start, just as I had. This was truly a man to be reckoned with on many levels.

It made me even more intent on winning and winning my way.

"Apology accepted, Randolph," I demurred. "So, if Silvia isn't to your liking, perhaps we should determine what it is you do want."

He looked at me through hooded eyes, his voice suddenly husky, "I thought that it was obvious."

"Manx. Control of the company." I was playing coy. I knew what he meant.

"No, Susan. I think you are fully aware that you are what I want. I think that sometimes you are overly transparent in your methods of distraction, but in the end, they do work. I think you are wonderful, body and mind. I have thoroughly enjoyed all our sport, but I am tired of games."

It was a longer speech than I expected.

"Randolph, you must know that I find you attractive. You probably also know that I have no long-term relationships because I quickly grow bored."

He started to speak again, to protest, but I put a finger up to stop him.

"That being said, I find you invigorating and challenging. In all honesty, you are the only man ever to impress me, to match me." I paused for emphasis before continuing.

"I believe that you are my match, that you are even stronger, smarter, and more aggressive than I am. I doubt you would ever bore me. I believe that, together, we are a force that could not be stopped." Again, I paused. I took a sip of water, and then went on.

"That is why I propose we form a partnership."

It took a moment for him to realize that I was done. He looked bewildered and a little hurt.

"I am not interested in a business associate, Susan." He bit out the words, straightened his shoulders, and lifted his chin to show that though feeling wounded, he still had his pride.

"Who said anything about business, Randolph," I replied, equally as coolly.

His eyes widened, just slightly, then a small smile started playing about his lips. I waited for him to make the first move. He did. Point to me.

Coming to me at my desk, he took my hand, examined my wrists, looking for bruises, kissed them gently, then took me in his arms, kissing me along my neck and to my mouth.

I wasn't in the least disappointed. He was as skilled in his lovemaking as he'd been in everything else.

Randolph lowered his zipper and pulled out his magnificent cock. He pushed my dress off my shoulders and I allowed it to fall and pool at my feet. He lifted me up in his powerful hands, cupping my bottom and spreading my thighs. I wrapped them around his narrow waist, putting my arms around his broad shoulders. He nestled the head of his cock in my wetness, then slowly pulled me to him, inch by inch pressing me onto his rigid hardness.

Our eyes met, his lustful, mine shining with desire. He lifted me again, just as slowly as before, and lowered me again.

For an eternity, we joined, then broke apart again. It was incredible. The power and control he showed, we showed. The sheer physical demands of this slow, inexorable lovemaking. I came in waves, convulsing in his hands and around his cock. But Randolph wasn't yet done. He withdrew and lifted me up to my desk. Raising my ankles up high in the air, he held my slender legs one-handed as he guided himself into me.

He still kept total control. His strokes were a little faster. The fingers of his left hand toyed with my clit. I came again and still he was solid inside me.

My phone chimed. I looked a question at Randolph. He nodded. I pressed the speaker button.

It was Tim, one of my research people. "I don't know if it's any use," he said, "but people close to Randolph Stone call him 'Tiger.' Some coincidence, huh?"

"Thanks, Tim. I already knew that, but thanks anyway." I clicked off.

Randolph looked down on me. "You knew they called me 'Tiger'?"

"No," I said, "not before. But I knew it, instinctively, by the way you've bested me, the way you've handled me. You've won, Randolph. Everything."

"I always do." And with that, he came.

Only a Tiger can tame a Tigress, but in our state, everything becomes joint property upon marriage.

Point. Match. Game to me.

O. Preston Telford

Every man's wet dream, but then again, I always have
said that what I want more than anything is another
woman or two around the house.

Open House

Moira was twenty-five and I was thirty when we got married. We were both doing well and we both had savings. She was assistant manager of Human Resources in a plant that employed four hundred people. I managed a thriving insurance brokerage. We agreed to buy the biggest house we could possibly swing. Real estate is the best investment there is, if you live in it and keep it long term.

It was tougher than we thought it'd be. The mortgage meant we couldn't hire any help. A four-thousand-square-foot home with a pool, sitting on an acre, is a lot of work. Moira'd get home about six-thirty. With me, it could be any time from six till nine or even ten. We shared the cooking and cleaning and yard work but all that vacuuming, dusting, polishing, and then the pool to tend, the lawn to mow or clear leaves from or shovel snow off and the planting and weeding . . . It was putting a strain on us, particularly on our love life. Most of the time, we were too fucking pooped to fuck.

There were nights when we'd start to fool around on the couch or somewhere but before we got past the foreplay, one or the other of us fell asleep. I was beginning to think we should sell our house to save our marriage, when Gemma, Moira's college roomie, broke up with her husband.

Gemma was like a sister to Moira. They totally looked alike, but where Moira was slender Gemma was shapely. Not fat, mind you, just nicely curved, with cushiony hips and lush boobs.

33

The main difference between them was that where Moira was ambitious and career-minded, Gemma was more of a homebody who loved to cook and clean and all that domestic stuff. Gemma could have had a high-powered job like Moira. She had the education, she just didn't have the desire. She hated the day-in-and-day-out grind of commuting to an office to deal with the backstabbing only to make a drive home and then try to put together a decent meal.

She loved to cook and was damn good at it, so she'd tried for a couple years to convince her now ex-husband that they would both be happier if she took care of cooking and the home and he worked. He had made enough to do it and she had worked at a small nonprofit barely making minimum wage. She had taken the job hoping it wouldn't be as much of a rat race there but it was almost as bad with the bickering and gossiping. Moira had told me on more than one occasion that the marriage would fail if he didn't get a clue about Gemma and so it had.

One night, about six months after Gemma and Bob had split, Moira snuggled up to me in the dark of our bedroom on our king-sized bed and started making little circles on my chest with her fingertips. "Jack," she said, "all this housework is killing us."

"I know," I agreed. "I've been thinking maybe we should sell and move into a condo."

"What if there was another way? What if we could reduce our debt and get some help around here?"

"Did we win a lottery?"

"No." She licked the side of my chest. "Jack?"

"Yes, darling?"

"Gemma's pretty well fixed. She got the house and a cash settlement and some nice alimony."

"Good for her."

"But she's lonely."

"She should get a boyfriend."

"Maybe, but if she marries again, she'll lose her monthly check. Jack?"

"Yes?"

Her fingers slipped into the fly of my boxers and toyed with my shaft. That's cheating, and she knows it. No using my cock to make decisions. We'd agreed to that a long time ago when the bugger kept getting us into trouble with his poor reasoning skills. But I didn't object this time, particularly when she tugged the sheet off us. She always does that if she's going to go down on me. Moira doesn't like having her head under the bed-clothes.

"We've got five bedrooms and three bathrooms upstairs, and there's just the two of us," she continued, stroking me idly. "What if Gemma sold her house and used some of the money to pay our mortgage down?" She wriggled down the bed and rested her cheek on my belly so that she was talking to my cock more than to me. "If she lived here, we'd have more disposable income and she'd cook and clean and do most everything except for the heavy work, and we'd be able to hire someone for that. You and I would have more time and energy for this sort of thing." Her lips closed around my cock, just below its head. "Mm?" she asked.

When I didn't answer right away she took my cock out of her mouth and drew a breath, as if to continue trying to talk me into agreeing. I, of course, very quickly said, "I think that's a great idea," and pushed down on the back of her head. I added, "You've discussed this with Gemma?"

Moira nodded, which was just fine by me.

Everything worked out pretty much as Moira said, but better. I got a good breakfast every morning instead of picking up coffee and a doughnut on the way to the office. There was a hot meal waiting every evening, and Gemma really was a great cook.

We got a pool service and a yard man, so most summer Sundays all the three of us did was hang around the pool, sipping our nice cool drinks, soaking up the sun, and them, in their tiny little suits, oiling one another up with me pretending not to watch from behind my sunglasses but often needing to cool down in the water or roll over to avoid an uneven tan, so to speak.

Most evenings, after a wonderful meal, we'd all change from our less comfortable work and day clothes into nightwear. For me, that was a robe and boxers. Moira wore wraps or negligees, silk pj's or flimsy baby-dolls. Gemma, like me, had to be more modest and always wore a robe but often with little or nothing beneath it. Inevitably, I caught accidental glimpses from time to time—the flash of a shapely thigh, an immodest amount of cleavage, or sometimes even the momentary display of a berry-brown nipple.

There were many nights when I took the erection Gemma had given me to bed for Moira to tend.

Our relatively innocent ménage had continued for about six months when one night in bed Moira started stroking my chest. I reached for the light because I like to see what, and who, I'm doing.

She said, "No," and pulled my arm down.

"Why not?" I asked.

"I have a confession to make and I do that better in the dark."

"Okay. What is it?"

She snuggled close, so that I could feel her breath on my ribs, and went on stroking my skin. My Moira can play me like a piano. I wouldn't have her any other way.

"Jack," she whispered, "when Gemma and I were in school, we were very close."

I shrugged. "You were always like sisters."

"I mean, even for roomies and best friends, we were extra

close." Her fingertips settled on the fly of my boxers. "We told each other everything."

"Such as?" I asked.

One of her fingers slipped through my fly and made little circles on my belly. "Well, we shared a room—two single beds. Sometimes, after one of us had been on a date, we'd cuddle up in one bed and talk about it."

"What's wrong with that?" I asked.

"We'd share intimate details. I'd tell her, 'I let Peter kiss me tonight, with tongues.' Or she'd tell me, 'Roger played with my tits tonight and it really got me hot.' Things like that."

My cock rose to greet the finger that was tracing lines on my skin. "That all sounds innocent to me," I said.

"This isn't my confession, silly. This is leading up to it."

"Oh. So?"

"Sometimes, when a girl isn't ready to go 'all the way' with a boy, after a heavy date, she's left pretty horny."

"Just like the boy is," I put in.

"And when a girl is very horny, and she's in bed with her sweet friend, and they're talking about sex and stuff . . . Well, you know." Her finger and thumb closed on my cock's shaft. Her free hand tugged the bedclothes aside.

"You? You and Gemma? You made out?" I croaked, with a mental picture of my slender young wife kissing her lush and lovely friend. "Er, what, exactly . . . ?"

Moira gave my cock a long slow stroke. "Fingers, mainly. You know, to get each other off."

"And that's your confession? Don't feel guilty, Moira. I bet lots of college women experiment with each other. It doesn't mean anything bad."

"Well, no, that's not my confession. Like I said, I'm leading up to that."

My throat went dry. My cock twitched between Moira's fingers. She pulled it out of my fly and continued, with all of her fingers stroking me.

"Jack, remember last Thursday, when you had to work late?"

I nodded in the dark.

"Gemma and I shared a bottle of wine, not that that's any excuse. We got to talking about old times and how we shared confidences. The topic got around to you and I boasted about what a good kisser you are."

"Thanks."

"And Gemma asked for a demonstration."

"And you kissed her—the way I kiss you?"

"And I told her how it is when you play with my nipples."

"And you demonstrated?" By then, my cock was hard, hot and throbbing.

"Yes. And then I told her how clever your fingers are, between my legs."

"And . . . ?"

"Yes. But I told her that your tongue was even better, when you lick me so nicely."

"And you . . . ?"

"Yes, and so did she, me. Jack, are you ashamed of me? Can you forgive me? I do love you and I'd never make love to another man, but . . ." Even as she begged my forgiveness, her fingers were working on my cock. Again, breaking the rules, but I wasn't about to point that out.

I gave my wife a squeeze. "Of course I forgive you, sweetheart. You didn't do anything you need forgiving for."

She said, "Thank you."

I felt the familiar sweet sensation of a pair of feminine lips closing over the head of my cock. For a moment I was confused. My wife's lips were kissing my chest, so . . .

I said, "Hi Gemma! That's nice, very nice, but why don't we turn the light on?"

That was a year ago.

Meanwhile, Gemma and Moira's college tutor, Elaine, who is a few years older than they are, left her job and contacted them to announce her intention to move to our city. She's about thirty-three and recently lost her boyfriend in a motorcycle accident. She told them she needed a change of scenery, a change of work, a change of everything. Elaine and I have met a few times at reunions and she's a bookish girl whose photo should be in the encyclopedia under "Geek Chic" cause there's just something about her glasses, her ponytails, her natural, no make-up look that makes a man have serious library fantasies.

Last night, I lay in bed with Gemma kissing my neck and her left breast filling my hand. Moira's cheek was resting on my thigh. Her breath was stirring the hairs on my balls.

Gemma said, "Jack?"

Moira continued, "About Elaine."

Gemma added, "She's been so lonely and devastated by losing Guy in that horrible accident."

Moira lifted her head to plant a kiss on the underside of my shaft. "We were thinking, if she sold off all her things and came to live here, we could pay off our mortgage completely and we'd be in a position to . . ."

I tapped her lips with the head of my cock to stop her. "Okay," I said. "Elaine is more than welcome. By the way, can this bed fit four, just in case?"

I felt a slap, then heard a giggle. I figured we'd fit four just fine.

Marcy Rosewood

Revenge is not best served up cold. Revenge is best when it's torrid.

Getting Her Move On

I placed two boxes on the bedroom floor, then unbuttoned my shirt and took it off. I wasn't trying to show off, though the weekend moving jobs kept my muscles toned. I was just hot and figured that my arms were a better sight than sweat soaking through my clothes.

Dee followed me into the bedroom. She seemed different than most women I worked for, and I liked that about her. She wasn't intimidated by my black skin or broad chest. She was real sweet, much less formal. Didn't treat me like the help but like a person. She wouldn't have a drink or a snack without offering me one, too.

"What the hell?" Dee exclaimed as she swept into the room. I thought at first she was upset about my naked chest, but that wasn't it. To the side of the unmade bed mattress was a small night table adorned with an alarm clock, a telephone, and a few framed photographs.

I had no idea what the problem was. But, from the way she snapped open her cell phone, I figured it must have been damn serious.

"Roger," she said through gritted teeth. I recognized her boyfriend's name. "Why did you take the right side of the bed?"

She tapped her foot while he answered. I tried not to stare, but I couldn't help myself. Her face is really pretty with green eyes and nice lips. And her body. Wow! She had on a thin white tank top, like a wife-beater, but with some sparkly things on it. It really emphasized her body . . . her breasts . . . her body. When she tossed her long black hair over her shoulder, my eyes dropped to her thin waist, her shapely hips, and thicker thighs. I bet those thighs could damage a man.

"But we agreed that I'd get the right side. I told you I can't sleep on the left." Dee walked to the room's only closet door and spread it open. Then, she gasped so hard that she almost swallowed the phone.

"Roger, you took up the whole closet? The entire thing?" She began shuffling through the clothes-draped hangers. "Holy shit. You hung everything up but your underwear and socks. Where are my clothes supposed to go?" she whispered, then shot me a stare that said I'd better leave her alone.

I went back to the hall for more. It was going to be a tough day. My partner hadn't shown up, and, although we'd taken care of all the heavy stuff the day before, I'd have to tend to a mountain of boxes and bags on my own.

It was definitely a move up for Dee. She was going from a small apartment below sidewalk level into a spacious, twelfth-floor space with a city view that was probably worth half the rent. It was her piece of the suburban pie. Perfect for a young woman with a golden smile.

Not so great for a guy like me. The suspicious glances that her new neighbors gave me suggested that I was the only black man in the building, maybe the only one on the whole street.

From what she'd been telling me on our shared elevator rides, Dee was moving in with some guy named Roger she'd been dating for a few months. He'd hired his own movers last night and had settled himself into their new place.

I was carrying a couple small boxes in one arm and a green plastic garbage bag in the other when I heard Dee scream. With boxes everywhere, some half unpacked, I figured she might have fallen on something and been hurt. I dropped what I was carrying and raced to the rescue.

Moments later, I found her in the master bathroom. She'd stopped screaming and was standing upright. But her left palm was clasped over her mouth as she peeked through the split fingers of her right hand.

"Look at this!" She invited me into the room.

The medicine cabinet was open and packed tight with the expected sundries along with expired prescription-drug containers, rusty disposable razors, and hair-packed brushes. A toothpaste tube had been left uncapped allowing a stream of paste to dry on the counter. Near it was a small, neat pile of what looked like fingernail clippings.

"Can you believe this?" she asked me.

"No." I really couldn't. I mean, I wasn't a neat freak, but they hadn't even officially moved in yet and it looked like Roger had spent last evening marking out his territory. My theory was confirmed when Dee flipped open the toilet lid. And screamed again.

"He didn't even flush!" She turned her neck away from the sight and used her shoe's toe to flip down the handle. She was on the phone again soon after.

"Is Roger there?" Her face turned so red that I considered calling some paramedics. The next minute all I could hear was her side of the conversation mixed with brief, silent pauses.

"Who answered your phone, Roger?" She cleared her throat.

"It sounded like that old girlfriend of yours."

And, "What the hell are you doing with her?"

Then, she hung up the phone and mumbled several words that it was probably better I didn't hear. After that, I followed her around through the rest of the apartment. Nearly every room, floor, or wall found another of her boyfriend's markings. In the dining area he'd hung a sixteen-month calendar topped with near-naked blondes with breasts that could have doubled as emergency flotation devices. He'd packed the refrigerator with beer, an empty bottle of ketchup and a paper bag of fast-food scraps. He'd put an ashtray on the balcony but stamped out a pack's worth of cigarette butts on the stained wooden deck.

Worst of all, he'd left a couple beer mugs on the deck's rail—one with a pink lipstick circle on its rim. From the way Dee began stomping and slamming and shouting after seeing that lipstick color, it was probably the trademark of Roger's ex-girlfriend. Who, maybe, wasn't so much of an "ex" after all.

A nasty smile took over Dee's lips as she turned to me. Her eyes scanned my chest, my arms, down my stomach, lower. I suddenly felt like a piece of meat. But it wasn't a bad feeling. I didn't mind at all.

With a smirk, she took a few steps toward me, swishing her hips as she walked. She looked like a woman on a mission. And I was the savage she expected to convert.

I could have declined. I could have reminded her that it's never a good idea to mix business and pleasure. Or even revenge and sex. But I'm a man. A straight man who has trouble saying no to a beautiful woman. That's how I got in the moving business in the first place. Finally decided to get paid for moving good-looking women around the city instead of doing it like a sucker for free.

I liked taking my time with these things, generally, but it only took Dee a few seconds to get completely naked. I wanted to run my mouth all over her smooth body. But she wanted different. Dee pushed me out backward onto the deck, unzipping my fly as she went. There, she dropped to her knees and pulled out my cock. Her mouth, warm and wet, quickly worked me to a hard-on. It was strange being so exposed like that. Out in the open. If she had a nosy neighbor, they'd see everything.

Suddenly she popped up and pulled me close for a wet kiss. Before I could open my eyes, we were back inside the apartment. She looked for a comfortable spot, settling for the dining room's hardwood floor. Dee dropped onto the cold surface and spread her legs open. With her hands on her inner thighs and her ankles high in the air, I guessed she didn't believe in subtlety, but again, I wasn't complaining.

I groaned when I entered her. She was wet but so tight. I moved slowly, worried that I would hurt her. Her nails digging into my backside and her high-pitched moans in my ear urged me on.

After a few thrusts, she tapped my shoulder. I thought, "Is this chick serious? She can't be finished already."

"Do me on the dining table." Her back arched and arms pushed until we were standing.

I glanced at the table—still covered with boxes. I reached around, picked her up by the ass and carried her to the kitchen counter.

"Good enough," she laughed while kissing my cheek, then my lips as she wrapped her long legs around my waist. I marveled at the way her pale thighs clashed with my dark skin. Rock hard, I was more turned on than ever before. Leaning back, she watched my cock slide into her.

But soon, she wanted to move on to the living room. First, we were on the sofa. Then on the new rug, a gaudy pistachio mess that her boyfriend bought. From there, it was "stop-and-go" fucking. Another room, then another as she re-marked the apartment with her own scent, mixed with mine.

A part of me was getting annoyed. I wasn't her personal fuck toy. Who did she think she was? Then again, a bigger part of me said, stop complaining. She was the finest woman I'd been with in a long time and, I'll admit, the way she moved kept me hard and wanting.

"For real this time." Dee must have sensed my frustration. She took my hand and led me to the bedroom, their bedroom. She lay back on the bare mattress while her fingers and lips summoned me to her.

I traced her curves with my tongue as her fingers roamed my body, palms massaging my muscles. I hooked her ankles over my shoulders, pushed her legs all the way back. I filled her with slow thrusts at first. Barely moving my hips, enjoying the way her eyes got wide. She moaned when I hit her in the right spot. I figured out that's what she liked most and gave it to her over and over. Pretty soon she was screaming so loud that my ears started to ring. I'm sure her new neighbors couldn't be happy about that.

When she came, she grabbed me by the neck, pulled me close. Her tongue went in my mouth at the same time my cock shuddered and spewed. I groaned into her mouth, feeling her tremble beneath me.

I collapsed to her side as her head snuggled into my chest and one leg draped across my lap. It took a few minutes of silence for our breath to steady.

"Have enough energy left to move my things back out?" she broke the mood.

"Sure," I returned. "Everything except the big and heavy stuff. But where does it go?"

"Damn," she thought out loud. "My family's a few states away and the lease on my old place is up tomorrow. The new tenant is already moving in."

She rubbed one leg up to my stomach while a finger played

with my chest. Her body molded to mine like she was at ease. Like we'd always been lovers. It wasn't a bad feeling at all. I didn't realize how much I missed something like this.

After taking a deep breath, I made a leap. "You could stay at my place. Temporary like. Until you get settled." I'd never lived with a woman before. Maybe it was time. "I have storage space in the garage. Two full bathrooms. Master bedroom has a walk-in closet I hardly use. Just a few suits."

I was selling her on it, hard. I don't know why, but I wanted her to move in and I wanted her, again, just this time all over my stuff in my place.

"What side of the bed do you sleep on?"

"The left. Always." It was the truth.

"Drink beer?" she snapped, fast.

"Not often. I tend to drink water to stay hydrated or like a little scotch sometimes. I always have a bottle of cabernet around, though. I like wine with dinner, which I can cook."

"Know how to flush a toilet?" her quiz continued.

"Of course!" It hadn't been an issue since I was a kid.

She snuggled into my arms, sighed softly, then whispered in my ear, "I'll take it, and I'll take you, too. Both sound perfect."

Neil Truitt

What is it about the threat of imminent death that drives us to our basest instincts, our need to fuck? Not that I wait around for a near-death experience or anything.

Sucking Wind

I'd been off the highway for an hour driving along lonely, desolate roads surrounded by flat, brown dirt and weedy fields. I was pretty sure I was still in Oklahoma, but other than that, I was lost. The road I was on, long and straight like an arrow, didn't seem to be leading anywhere. Other than an occasional, modest home, I passed mainly carpets of dry, ankle-high weeds, sparsely broken up by small stands of trees. I loved it. I loved the wide openness of the landscape. It was completely different from the boxed-in cities I'd always lived in. Cities were suffocating me but here, here, a man could breathe again.

Suddenly, hard taps began hitting the car roof, and the windshield blurred as olive-sized hail rained down. The weather hadn't seemed too bad moments before, and I figured this was just some sort of freak storm. But then I saw a shape I recognized from news reports and movies—a funnel with a thin and dancing root spiraling upward into a darkness that gobbled the sky. And I heard the rush of what sounded like a freight train, but there weren't any tracks around.

A tornado.

I marveled at the sight. This was exactly the reason I was driving across country rather than flying. Quickly though, my curiosity quelled as the tornado seemed to turn and make a wild dash straight at me.

I slammed the gas and the car chugged and gasped before it spat down the road. I didn't know where I was going, but I was going there in record time. Soon, a house sprung up along the road. I pulled into its dirt driveway, kicking gravel up behind as I spun around a tall tree with twisted limbs and burnt green leaves.

There were two women near the house. The shorter one, in a red bathrobe, had magnificently long hair, blacker than the night. Native American, I thought. Though I think now that you're supposed to call them Indian again if you don't know their correct tribe because how can they be natives of America when America didn't exist.

Her heart-shaped face with apple cheeks glowed with a healthy tan and her bathrobe couldn't hide her shapely figure. In just that quick look, I could see that her body was supple, graceful, and that it seemed to move even when she stood still.

I glanced behind her to the taller woman with sparkling red lips. She was lithe, like she'd spent some time on the fashion runway, and had dainty features on top of a swanlike neck. She wore jeans with a dusk yellow blouse that matched the color of her long, wavy hair.

They'd spotted the tornado, and my car, heading their way and anxiously motioned for me to join them. I slapped into park and, on foot, caught up to them in the side yard near a metal bulkhead set flat against the ground. The taller one struggled with the door's handle, forcing it to slowly creak open—as though it hadn't been used in years. Beneath was a ladder leading into a dark, underground chasm.

"In! Quick!" They chimed together. Their urgent words were enough to propel me forward and down.

The ladder groaned under my weight, but it was short, and before I expected my feet stomped on hard concrete. Inside, the walls were made of unworked stone held together with mortar so old that the slightest touch turned it into dust. The place was the size of a garden shed but with a lower ceiling, little more than enough room for the three of us to stretch.

When the taller woman pulled the door closed behind her, we were swallowed by thick darkness.

"Shouldn't last long," one of them said, but I hadn't figured out their voices yet.

"Bad idea," I gulped. In the haste, I'd forgotten how much I hated tight places. For me, they were just like the city—smoggy, stifling, suffocating. I moved so I was closest to the door, then said, "I'll have to wait outside. I'll lie down, or something."

Strong fingers grabbed my shirtsleeve. "It's heading right for us."

"Outside is suicide," the other insisted as what sounded very much to me like a subway train rolled closer. The relentless noise became louder and louder, shaking the dusty mortar off the walls and causing our protective metal door to quiver.

"Sorry." My shaking matched that of the door. "I . . . I can't stay. I'm claustrophobic. Can't take these closed-in places. I can't breathe." I coughed into my sweaty palm and then wheezed to prove the point.

"If that door opens, it could kill us all," an anonymous voice whispered. She was right. And I struggled to care. My mind coached me to wait out the wind, but my body screamed for open air. Suddenly, a gush forced the door to quake and then to bow out as though a strong magnet was pulling it up. The sound of our breathing mixed, then held.

The door, that thin slice of metal separating us from the tornado, was about to break open.

I jumped.

"Don't!" A scream followed me as I leaped onto the ladder,

grabbed the door's handle, and pulled down with all my weight. I didn't want to be in there. But I wasn't going to waste the lives of people who shared their safe spot with me.

The door jerked violently, banging against the frame and forcing my body to snap repeatedly upward and down. My heart thumped while my lungs gasped for sweet, fresh air. I screamed loud and long, hoping the noise would scare the whirlwind away. I didn't know how long I could hold that door before I just let it sail all of us away.

And then I felt a warm hand on my thigh.

I didn't know which one of them it was. I could barely see a form below me in the darkness. She started rubbing gently along my pants, up until she reached my crotch and cupped my balls through the cloth. Her other hand moved quickly to my fly. Unzipping it, her fingers reached inside, searching for my cock. She found it, growing hard.

I didn't understand how I could be aroused then, in that dark, closed room with death pounding at the door above. But my cock had sprung to life, damning the circumstances—if not to survive, then for one, final performance.

The hand snuck my erection out and then warm lips engulfed me as her tongue tip darted along the underside of my shaft. I imagined, first, that it was the shorter woman with her tousled black hair. Then, I dreamed of the other with her eyes closed and nipples hard.

For a moment, my mind danced between their images and I was almost able to forget all about the storm and being trapped. I wanted to reach down to feel the hair on the back of her head. But the door shook so violently that I dared not let go.

She stopped, and I heard the shuffling of fabric. I blinked rapidly, trying to adjust my eyes to the darkness, but to no avail.

Warm lips wrapped around my cock, a tongue flicking my head, as an extra pair of hands reached over and steadied my thigh.

It was both of them.

Again the wind kicked high, forcing my body to jerk wildly even as my cock writhed between the hidden lips. Before, claustrophobic fears and wild, terrified emotions had trashed my mind. Now, my subterranean friends were helping me to focus on holding on to the bucking door. Helping me to focus on my excruciatingly hard cock.

One, maybe it was the shorter one, tugged my pants down several inches. Her hand first touched the base of my cock, then began caressing my balls. Just when I was about to come, I think they exchanged some kind of signal and switched places. Fresh lips licked me slowly, cautiously like she wanted to take her time. Grazing my tip with her lips, licking the sides of my cock, she enjoyed me fully, all while tickling and taunting my balls.

When I let out a low, joyful moan, palms clasped onto my ass and I felt the head of my cock being sucked into her throat. Wedged tight, she gagged at my first gush, then took the rest easily as fingernails dug into my backside. The other one moved in to lick my sensitive head, tasting the last traces and sucking me deep into her mouth.

By the time they moved back and away, the wind had nearly stopped and my breath was calm. Arms sore and palms cramped, I barely had enough energy to tuck myself back in my pants.

Figuring it was probably safe, I pushed open the door and climbed out of our cave. After taking a deep breath, I offered my hand to help them outside.

I was embarrassed by my fear. I didn't want people to know. I fought my whole life to keep it under control, under wraps. And, here, I'd lost it in front of two very attractive strangers.

Almost as bad, I didn't know which one I should thank first. If they hadn't calmed me down with their warm lips, I'd have probably been torn apart by the tornado.

"You were very brave," the tall one moved in and kissed my right cheek. Quickly, the shorter one moved in and kissed the other.

"I have to go," I was rude in my brevity, but I couldn't face them, couldn't look them in the eyes. My words were followed by several moments of awkward silence.

"You can't," said the taller one.

"She's right," the other agreed.

"I have an appointment. I'm sorry." I looked at my wrist, forgetting that I wasn't wearing a watch. I wanted to stay, but it was time I went.

"You don't get it," the shorter woman grabbed my elbow, "you cannot go."

I was trying to pull away and starting to worry about what I'd gotten myself into when she let go and used her free hand to point. She pointed toward my car.

It didn't bother me that the passenger door was heavily dented. It wasn't even a real big deal that the back windshield was shattered. No. The big problem was that my car was parked upside down and twenty feet high in the gnarled branches of the front yard's tree.

She was right. I couldn't go. But I figured, based on their matching smiles as I turned back to them, that I could come.

Elizabeth Claire

Did you ever have major fantasies about using the bench and thigh press at the gym for something a little more recreational? I did.

Breaking a Sweat

I was stretching my legs when Janice entered the gym. She flashed her dimples and bounced toward me. "Hey, Michelle. Haven't seen you around."

Had she been looking for me? I grinned as I admired the way her shorts showed off her lean thighs and said, "Been slammed with work."

"I know how that is. I thought maybe you decided to go to a real gym."

"And leave all this behind?" I swept my arms toward the barely used machines. With a sweet giggle that I really liked, though it was very girly, she went to the lone treadmill to warm up.

When I first moved into my condo, I had checked out their "fitness center." What a laugh. It was barely above my old high school's weight room. It was not particularly impressive with the single treadmill, some free weights, and an all-in-one weight machine from the '70s. I was unimpressed, but at the same time figured I would have plenty of time to myself as I doubted it was used much. Also, I really liked the condo, it was in a great area, and I wasn't going to pass up on it just over some crappy old equipment.

Once I'd moved in, I noticed that no one really used the gym. A few older residents every now and again and some early birds. After ten or so, the room was almost always empty, which was perfect for me and much better than going to a crowded gym. Once, I dropped by the closest gym, and it was a total meat market. Not my kind of place in more ways than one. When I work out, that's all I want to do for the most part. I don't need some musclehead hitting on me or crowding my machine.

So, overall, the tiny gym was good enough. Thirty minutes on the treadmill followed by another half hour of free weights then a ten-minute cooldown on the mat and I could do it all uninterrupted and without some news program blaring or electronica blasting from the kickboxing classes.

Today, however, Janice was there to work out, too. She showed up to work out about the time I was leaving the first few weeks I was here, then started coming a little earlier. I also had started staying a bit later. I don't know why she changed her schedule, but I knew why I had as I watched Janice's slender legs moving back and forth. She wasn't really my type: a little too petite for my tastes. I'm a curvy girl, and I worry about being too much for the smaller ladies.

Still there was something about her that caught my attention. Maybe it was the combination of her jet-black hair and almost translucent skin. Too pretty to be a Goth, and with her giggle and bouncing about, she lacked the suicidal attitude, but I still imagined her dressed all in black and reading poetry by candlelight.

I saw Janice glaring at the Behemoth. That's what she called the ancient weight machine that took up the center of the gym. It was tall, clunky, and completely worthless. Dangerous, no doubt, and rusted in areas. It had arms like a praying mantis and so many round weights attached to it that it resembled the storage area of a tire store.

"It gets uglier every time I see it."

She wrinkled her pert nose. "I can't stand it. I've written to the condo association, but they still haven't gotten rid of it."

"I bet they could fit two new machines in its place. Cheap bastards."

"If I could drag it out of here, I would. I can't stand old things."

"Hey, now. That's not something you say in front of an older woman." I still consider myself young, but I had more than a few years on her.

She laughed. "You're not old." She kicked the machine. "But this crap is."

I sat down on the behemoth's padded seat and looked up at her. She had such a slim waist. I wanted to pick her up and put her on my lap. Instead I said, "I take it that you're not a big fan of antiques."

"I hate them. My parents ran a little antique shop. Seemed like everything was made of dust."

I scooted over so she could sit next to me, if she wanted. She did, swinging a leg over so she straddled the bench and faced me.

I was surprised her parents weren't lawyers or stockbrokers. I'd assumed she came from real money. She was a sucker for luxury labels, so I figured she'd been born with a platinum spoon in her mouth.

Now that I knew she hadn't, I liked her a bit more. She must work hard to afford her condo and all her nice things. That made her a go-getter, someone who saw something they liked or wanted and did what needed to be done to get it.

She smiled, her knees pressing against me. They poked hard into me, but I imagined the rest of her was much more pliable.

Her pink lips looked moist. "I guess we'd better get back to working out."

"Right." Her face was just inches away from me, but I didn't dare. After learning a tidbit of her past, I still didn't know enough about her to go in for the kiss. Also, I'd made the mistake before of assuming some friendly chatting and a hug or two meant what I wanted it to mean. I didn't want to be that embarrassed again.

She surprised me again.

She leaned forward and kissed me. No questions, no hesitation. Just the sweetest kiss I've ever tasted. It was lips and tongue with a bit of teeth. It was a wrestling match that made me want to pin her to the mat for a ten count.

She reached inside the waistband of my shorts, but I stopped her. "Wait."

"What's wrong?" she asked.

I glanced up at the Behemoth. The machine seemed filthier than ever. "Doesn't that spoil the mood a little? Want to take it back to my place?"

She smiled, reached down to cup my breast, and squeezed. Her voice was husky when she said, "I can't wait."

Neither could I. I arched my back when she brushed my nipple with her thumb. I always figured she was a submissive. Maybe it was her dainty frame, the innocent tint in her eyes. She surprised me when she grabbed my wrists, put them over my head.

"Right where I want you," she said as she kissed me hard, nibbling my lower lip. Not only what she was doing but what she'd said about wanting me sent shock waves from my cunt to my toes.

She tugged my sports bra down to my stomach, then followed it with her mouth, moving down my neck, teasing my nipples and under my breasts, then along my stomach and back up to my nipples, where she sucked one right into her mouth and flattened it against the roof with her tongue. Her top teeth bit into it ever so slightly, then harder, then gently again as she pulled and sucked until I thought I'd come just from the attention she was paying to it.

She stopped, sensing how close I was, and said, "Not yet."

"You tease." I reached for her, but she pushed me down until my back was on the padded bench again.

Standing, she straddled my waist, balancing both hands on the Behemoth's hanging arms.

I admired her defined arms and the way her shoulders looked so toned. She grinned and took off her spandex top. She shook her chest at me and I so wanted to squeeze her dainty breasts, fit them in my palms, pull her down on top of me, and kiss her again.

She squatted a bit until her bottom barely grazed my stomach, not quite touching me. I put my hand between her muscular thighs. They were hard from years of leg presses and calf raises. "Nice," I told her.

"Thanks. Now give me your hands," she said.

I complied. I watched her tie my left wrist to one arm of the weight machine. She wouldn't be able to wear that sports bra again. Then she used my top to tie my right wrist. She worked quickly until I was bound to the machine.

"That's better," she said. With a swift motion, she pulled my shorts over my hips and down to my ankles and tossing my panties to the floor, she stood there. She allowed her eyes to wander all over my body, up and down. I felt like she was touching me the way she looked so intently at me, then the tip of her tongue licked her upper lip and I thought I could almost feel it on my clit and up inside my pussy. Again, I almost came just from her watching me and licking her own lips. I'd never felt like this before, but then I'd never been on the submitting side of things either.

Her fingers moved like silk between my legs. "Mmmm . . . I

like chicks with hair," she said as she wrapped a few of the longer curls about her fingers and pulled. I never will understand hairless pussies, not when the hair catches the slick wetness and it gives you something to grab, to pull, and to tug.

Before I could respond, she knelt in front of the bench, lifted my legs, and hooked them over her shoulders. She looked like a sexy imp, nestled between my thighs with her plump lips right over my wet lips.

Still staring at me, she dipped her mouth, lightly tasting me with the tip of her tongue. Even that soft touch made me jump. I wanted to cup her face, grind myself against her mouth. But I was helpless. Completely tied to the machine. Helpless, too, because I realized I would do anything she asked of me, anything at all to have her look at me the way she had.

"Sweet Michelle," she whispered. "You taste better than I'd ever expected."

I was amazed again that she'd been thinking of me, of how I might taste.

"Fuck me, please, fuck me with your hand," I begged.

I lost track of time. It was like she spent hours between my legs. Her mouth slowly savored every inch of me, her hot tongue exploring everywhere, first a finger, then finally her whole fist up inside of me, spreading me, bruising me, filling me entirely. When I came the second time, I wanted her to untie me. I wanted to dive between her legs and taste her juices. With a mischievous laugh, she refused. It was sweet torture.

Of course, throughout everything I had lost all track of time and place, which explains why I didn't notice that we had a small audience. When I opened my eyes, I noticed three men hovering in the background. Who knows how long they'd been standing there, but judging from how uncomfortable they looked in their clothes, I'd say long enough.

Janice played cool as she stood, wiping her mouth with the back of her hand. "Can we help you?" she asked.

The three men looked at each other. One opened his mouth, glanced at me, then changed his mind.

She put her hands on her hips. "Need something? If not, could you come back later?"

The tallest one took a shy step forward. "Ma'am, we're here to take care of the machine."

"The machine?" she asked.

He pointed at the Behemoth, but he couldn't keep his eyes off my nude, bound body. "The condo association said they've received complaints about that machine. No one uses it, so they hired us to take it away."

Janice and I shouted at the same time. "No! We use it!" She looked down at me, and we both burst out laughing.

After a second, the tall one looked at me and then looked at her, nodded his head before ushering his partners out of the gym, and said at the door, "We'll leave you two to finish your workout."

Janice beamed.

"I'm glad they left," I told her. "We should write the condo association, and tell them we want to keep the Behemoth."

"We can do that in the morning," she said.

I shook my wrists. "Now can you untie me?"

She pushed down her shorts and dropped them to the floor. She smiled and said, "I will, in a little bit. I want my workout first."

Then she worked out her thighs with some beautiful squats.

Olivia Ulster-Reed

JennaTip #3: Fisting

If you aren't careful, your hand could be broken while your partner orgasms and other facts you've never even thought to ask about fisting. Ways to avoid one of the weirdest reasons for having to wear a splint on your hand include breaking the vise-like vacuum grip on your wrist by gently pulling at her labia, pressing on her lower stomach gently, and finally, just relaxing your hand as much as possible and waiting it out.

Be careful with fisting. It sounds violent, but it isn't or at least doesn't have to be. Allowing someone inside you that deeply can be a very physically and emotionally amazing adventure. You may feel blissful, you may have intense orgasms, and you may cry and weep hysterically from feeling vulnerable and frightened. If it hurts, stop. If you are hurting someone, stop.

Finally, how to for those that want to:

1. Your partner must be highly aroused. Otherwise, the walls won't come tumbling down or in this case won't open up allowing you inside. Take your time and do it right.
2. Your partner must be relaxed. This is very much like the tips in *Something Blue* on anal sex. LUBE. LUBE. LUBE. RELAX. GO SLOWLY.
3. Wear a latex glove for protection from sexually transmitted diseases.
4. As mentioned above, start slowly with just one or two fingers at a time and with lots of touching and talking and kissing and relaxing.
5. Imagine trying to squeeze your hand out of a tight bangle bracelet or handcuff. (You know you've tried.)
6. Knuckles down, which is not the same as knuckle down. Assuming your partner is on her back, start with your knuckles facing down, then slowly rotate your hand as you press into the vagina. ADD MORE LUBE.

7. Have your partner breathe deep, relaxing breaths.
8. Let your hand curl up once inside. You can remain completely still, rotate your fist gently, push and pull, or a combination but keep in mind that very small movements will be enough. No grand gestures needed at this time.

Be aware that fisting can be an incredibly intense experience leaving your partner feeling vulnerable. Be certain that you are gentle, loving, and understanding with your partner throughout the entire experience.

Writer's Cramp (her version)

He told me how he sold everything and packed a bag with eight of his best scripts. He was on his way to Hollywood. Of course he was. I could've guessed that just from looking at him. He had that sweet puppy-dog look about him. I didn't want to see him after all the air was kicked out of him by a nasty pair of executive producer's shitkicking boots. But that's jumping ahead of the story.

He joined my bus in Detroit. In his rush to get to the back, he passed me without seeing me. I noticed him because I was bored, bored, bored.

I made a point of dangling my long leg out into the aisle, of letting my ballet flat dance on my big toe, waving the shoe about like a flag in the wind.

He had to notice. Everyone else did.

Chicago was a layover. I quickly got off the bus, then watched him as he hurried, trying to find me. I could see it in his face.

Good. He was bored, too. Bored and horny. My favorite kind of seatmate. Time for me to relocate to the back of the bus.

I waited, and when I climbed on board and sashayed my way back to the last row, I saw that most people were staking out entire rows and that after about two-thirds of the way, there was no one else but him. Perfect.

He was looking so sad and forlorn I couldn't help but smile. When he saw me, he flushed up to his scalp with happiness. I imagined making him flush that way with pleasure. God, but I'm a slut.

"Do you mind if I take the window seat?" I asked sweetly.

His eyes flickered across to the empty rows of seats.

"I like to ride on the right," I explained.

Mumbling something, he half stood to allow me through. It was a tight squeeze. I brushed against him as I wiggled through, then leaned back across to get a blanket and pillow from above, almost crushing his face into my aching breasts.

His cock reacted. I could tell because it felt like it reached out and slapped me, it got hard so fast, and he hurriedly covered his lap with his computer. I flipped the light off and slowly lowered myself to my seat.

"Writer?" I asked, looking at his screen. "Movie scripts, right?"

"Yeah. Trying."

"Me too. Not writing. I'm an actress, heading for Hollywood."

"Me too," he told me. "Hollywood. I'm Trent Porter."

"DeeDee Dahl. That's not my real name, of course. 'DeeDee' for double-D—get it?" I pulled my shoulders back.

"Yes, I get it."

"I'm hoping to be typecast as a dumb blonde."

"But you're not." He managed not to make it a question, barely.

"Master's degree in literature, bachelor's in drama."

"Wow."

"So, who do you know?"

He gave me a totally blank look. It was very sexy.

"Any contacts in Hollywood?"

Dawn broke on old marble head. "No."

"Me either. We must be mad, right?"

"Time will tell."

"If I take a nap, will it disturb you?" I smiled coyly.

He said it wouldn't, but I could see that just being within touching distance of me was disturbing him. I slumped back, pushing my feet forward, making my impossibly short skirt slide higher up my bare thighs. I rested the pillow against the window and put my cheek on it, then, turning away from him, I pushed my ass back so that it rested firmly against his thigh. I knew he was going to have a hell of a time sleeping, writing, or breathing with me like that. Just the knowledge that I could turn a perfect stranger on a bus into a gibbering fool got me wet. It was all I could manage to not finger myself right then and there. This bus ride wasn't going to be nearly so long and dull as I'd worried.

Eventually he must have relaxed as I could feel his leg stop trembling and knew he'd finally gotten his mind off my ass and his cock. That's when I rolled over, putting my head on his shoulder and allowing my hand to fall onto his thigh, almost in his lap. Then I fell asleep as I felt him stiffen, all of him stiffen.

Eventually, he dozed off. When he woke, I spoke without opening my eyes.

"It's two more days to LA. It could get very boring."

He grunted agreement.

"We could entertain each other," I suggested.

"How?"

"We could make out."

"For two days?" He looked around. The bus was mostly dark. "What about the other people?"

I giggled. "I don't want to make out with them."

Again with that hot blank look.

"Just kidding. No one can see us, can they? We could make out at night and nap by day." I licked my lips with the tip of my pink tongue. "And we've got a blanket."

I saw that he was finally getting my meaning. By make out I meant so much more than a few sweet tender kisses.

He managed an "Um" before I leaned up into him and kissed his dry but cute lips.

I'd chewed a few mints while he slept, so I knew my mouth was sweet and fresh. His, not so much.

"Here. Have a mint or six." I'm very resourceful.

"I've got more," I assured him. I don't know how assured he felt, what with getting a half dozen up front, but he really shouldn't eat onion rings if he's hoping to pick up a hot girl like me on a long bus ride.

Clearly his quick wit and exceptional personal hygiene were winning me over. He crunched three and got back to my lips, feeling confident enough to make a thorough exploration of my mouth. I could feel him hesitating to go further. So sweet. So I helped him along by taking him in hand, so to speak.

I placed my hand firmly on his crotch and then with my other guided his hand to my waist.

He gently started caressing my skin with his fingertips, sending little chill bumps all up and down my back and making my already hard nipples turn to aching stone. He moved slowly up, up, up to let the backs of his fingers brush the under curve of my right breast.

"My nipples," I confided, "are very sensitive."

My sweater was tight and he didn't have a lot of room to move, having to kind of scrunch down to get his arm up there. It was pretty cramped, but he wasn't deterred. See. I do have a degree in literature.

My lips trailed from his neck to his mouth. I was panting

minty clean breath and then I pushed my tongue fiercely in his mouth as he gradually applied more pressure to my nipple.

"Yes," I gasped into his mouth, so close to coming when suddenly he stopped. I pulled back to see what was up and his face was contorted with pain. I realized his hand was cramping and it must hurt like a fucking son of a bitch to actually cause him to pause. Then he fought it off, thank God, because I was worried I was with some pussy wimp who was going to fall apart on me before we'd even begun.

"We're stopping," I said as I noticed we'd pulled off the highway. "For now," I continued.

He worked his reluctant hand down and free, somehow adjusting his cock so that its head was trapped behind the buckle of his belt.

It was a two-hour stop. He got on first. Just before the bus left, I sashayed my sexy little self back to him, watching his eyes go to and fro like I was a tennis ball at Wimbledon. I had changed, of course, and was in a little denim skirt with a cropped zipper-front bomber jacket that was so adorable. These were my new, easier access, clothes. I didn't want any more hand cramps at inopportune moments.

It was a long, bright, sunny day and I could tell poor Trent was suffering, wishing for an eclipse or something to allow us to get back to our nighttime activities. At seven, I leaned over to him, breathing more than speaking into his ear, and told him, "Sunset's at eight-ten. You doing anything at about eight-twenty?"

He barely could nod, and smiling I went back to reading my mags. I am such a bitch. A sexy, cute, worth-it bitch, but a bitch nonetheless.

At eight, I turned off the light and got down the blanket and pillow again. He stroked me gently along my thigh as we waited for dark. At eight-nineteen I turned to him, pulled the blanket up to cover us to our throats, and whispered into his neck, "Remember where you were?" My jacket zipper was quite audible to us, but went unnoticed by our fellow travelers.

He remembered exactly and made good use of the open access the jacket provided. He cupped and squeezed my breast, weighing it in his palm, then finally getting down to business and pulling and rolling my nipple, tugging it and flicking the tip. Just as I thought I couldn't stand any more, he switched to my other nipple, giving it the same attention and more.

"God, Trent, I wish we were alone. They want to be kissed and sucked."

"I want to, Dee Dee. I do."

I reached for his other hand and pulled.

"I'm not wearing any panties."

"Oh." Clearly he intended to wow Hollywood with his gripping dialogue.

He slowly stroked upward as I parted my thighs. He quickly found my wet lips and still kissing me and kneading my tit, he went to work delving into me.

"Clit," I said right into his mouth.

I'm betting he'd never been with a girl like me who'd tell him right off where to go to get her off, but I wasn't wasting time.

Fingering my nipple, he sucked at my tongue and used his thumb to rhythmically compress the little pink nub between my pussy's lips until I jerked in his arms and sighed a breathy, "Thank you."

"My pleasure." And he meant it. Nice.

He held me for a bit, stroking my hair and kissing my forehead. He was clearly being sweet and trying to be a gentleman because I could feel the heat radiating off his aching crotch.

Eventually, I gave him a little kiss on the corner of his mouth, then turned and told him, "Your turn."

I should be a writer. He almost swooned at my words.

Unbuckling his belt, I unzipped him and felt around in his jeans until I worked his stiff johnson out. He was holding his breath, waiting to see what I'd do. I stood, peeked around to see if anyone could see, then told him to move to the window seat.

I turned to face the aisle, lifted my skirt, and sat on his lap, impaling myself on his cock, burning it up with my scalding juicy pussy.

"Keep still," I told him. "Play with my tits some more, please, Trent."

He did, under the cover of the blanket, tweaking and tugging them as I wriggled about on his lap. It wasn't enough for him to come but enough for him to be on the verge and it worked for me, bringing me to another lovely orgasm.

He tried to speak, but I cut him off.

"I know," I said as I managed to kneel down with my feet under the seat in front of us, putting me lips-to-cock with him. I pulled the blanket up over my head, wrapped my hand around his cock, then lowered my mouth onto his cock head.

He spread his thighs and the muscles stiffened. He felt under the blanket to touch my lips and face. I kept pumping him with my hand and mouth, occasionally stopping to lick him from balls to tip and back.

It didn't take long for him to come all in my mouth. I licked the last bit off my lips as I climbed back up next to him in the seat.

"Try to get a little sleep now," I said. "I promise I'll wake you in time for a quickie before dawn."

And I did. I woke him with my hand clamped around his nicely thickening cock, stoking him slowly to awareness. It was fun to watch his eyes open wide, then roll back in his head. I kept up the slow pace, giving him time to slip his hands between my thighs and his fingers inside my pussy. He tickled my clit and wiggled his fingers about really quite well and I was glad he wasn't having any more cramping trouble. Writers really do have dexterous hands, and the pads of his fingers had little calluses from thousands of keystrokes. I had a little bitty orgasm, then set my mind to it and had a nice big one that would have turned heads if I hadn't bit his shoulder to keep myself quiet. The act of biting him pushed him over the edge and he came in nice big globs of white all over my pretty hands.

He managed to get some work done during the day with only a few minor interruptions from me to chat. Then, at dark, we met again under the blanket. I hadn't changed. The outfit I had on gave him the best access and I was on a bus anyway, so didn't really need anything fresh until we arrived in Hollywood. The very thought made me so horny and wet. Hollywood. I swore the next time I came I'd yell Hollywood like a lover's name.

But right then, we were touching and playing and kissing. It was friendly and sexy and fun but after a few hours of this I had had enough. It was about one a.m. when I stood and invited Trent to come along. We slipped into the tiny, nasty bathroom and I managed to get his jeans and boxers down about his ankles because I'm really quite limber and except for my huge boobs, thin.

While I was down there, I decided to give him a little kiss. I tongued and sucked his cock and when I thought he was close to coming I stood, put my ass on the counter and spread my thighs for some good, old-fashioned bus-bathroom fucking.

"Fuck me, Trent." Fuck me, Hollywood!

Clasping my hands behind his neck, I pulled him to my breasts. Finally.

"Suck my tit, Trent," I hissed. "I've wanted you to do that since the moment we met."

So suck he did. And fuck we did. And of course, I managed to squeeze my hand between us and work my clit. I didn't yell "Hollywood," I thought it would be rude, so I thought it really, really loudly in my mind as I came.

We made our way back to our seats and spent most of the night contentedly kissing and cuddling. Just before dawn my hand went back to his cock. I jerked him off, this time being prepared with a yellow fast-food napkin to catch his jism.

At four in the afternoon we pulled into the bus station in LA.

"Do you have a cell-phone number for me?" he asked. "Or an address?"

Poor, sad little boy. Only in Hollywood for a few minutes and he was about to have his heart ripped right out of him, but I figured it was best to be up front and honest with him, since from that point forward I doubted anyone else in LA would ever be.

"It's been great fun, Trent," I said. "I've really enjoyed our trip together, but this is where our new lives start. From here on, I'm a starlet and you're a writer. I know I plan to play dumb blondes, but there isn't a blonde in Hollywood so dumb she'd fuck a writer."

And I was gone.

Isaac Andrews

Please park the car before loosening your seat belt, or any other belts for that matter!

Driving Blind

"Jack, this is Carol," my good friend Tom introduced. She was mid-twenties, a couple inches taller than me, and thinner than she had to be. It was hard to tell how attractive she really was, but I definitely got the impression she was. Her face was partly hidden by long strands of dark hair and wide-eyed glasses while most of her body was cloaked by a black trench coat that barely let her shins peek out of the bottom.

When our hands met for a shake, what she gave me was limp and cold. It was a brief touch before her arm dropped back down to her side.

I swore, right then, that this would absolutely be the last blind date I ever went on.

It was for a good cause, I supposed. Tom had been trying to get a date with Ashley for months. She was a bartender at the place we hung out to watch the games. Her nickname, one that even she answered to, was 3B for Blonde, Built, and Bad. She finally agreed to a movie date with him, as long as he made it a double for her friend Carol. I had lost a bet, so I was volunteered.

As though to tease me, at least that's the way I saw it, Ashley had dressed opposite from my date, wearing a thin, red blouse and suede miniskirt. Sure, the start was unexceptional, but maybe Carol was just shy. It had to get better. Right?

I drove us all to the movies. We'd somehow managed to agree to a remake of a not particularly inspired horror flick as the evening's entertainment. I'd pushed for playing pool or something more social, but had been outvoted. Ashley and Tom obviously wanted the dark anonymity of the movie theater and I was now more than happy to have something to distract me from my date, since she wouldn't even look at me during the entire ride.

Instead of responding to my polite overtures, Carol scrunched close to the passenger's side door and kept a steady watch outside the open window. Any of the get-to-know-you questions I'd asked her, she'd answered with a headshake, a nod or a shrug. Most of them required words, but she somehow managed to avoid anything that required an open mouth, as though she'd catch something if she parted her lips.

The backseat of my car was far more lively. Tom and Ashley laughed a lot and before we'd gotten a few miles down the road, they had a tight grip on each other's hands and had moved to meet thighs in the center of the seat.

In the theater, Tom and I sat on opposite ends with the women in the middle. The other two continued getting to know each other. They whispered and laughed. They brushed lips frequently and, not that I was spying on them, but I could have sworn she ran her fingers across his lap during a particularly dark scene.

Carol continued to be disinterested. She didn't want a soda. She refused candy and popcorn. She sat through the film with her legs crossed and her fist on her chin. The only words she said to me the entire time were, "Excuse me" as she scuttled across my knees on her sole trip to the restroom.

All of this was made worse because the movie wasn't worth the price of the tickets.

I didn't expect the ride back to be any better. Especially when Carol claimed she had a headache and wanted to go home, rather than grab a few drinks. She walked through the parking lot—a good twenty feet ahead of us. I didn't look forward to the ride to her place. And, as though headaches are contagious, I started getting one as well.

Carol went right back to her previous pose, cuddling against the door with her nose stuck toward the window. I promised myself that I'd focus on driving. I wouldn't even try to engage her in idle chitchat.

While the air in the front of the car was chilled and stale, the back was getting hot and heavy—even before we made it out of the parking lot. In the rearview mirror, I could see them from the chest up, and while there wasn't much happening that I could see, the sounds they were making left little to my imagination. There were a few giggles, some heavy breathing, a sharp intake of breath, and a sigh. Then some kissing that I could see and a long period of silence as Tom slowly liberated Ashley's shapely breasts from her blouse and bra. I couldn't see much because his arm and shoulder blocked my view and when he sat back, his hand covered a good part of it, though not all by any means. He'd have to be a pro ballplayer who could palm a basketball to cover the whole of her breast. I looked out the corner of my eyes at Carol to try to appraise how she compared, but the way she sat, hunched up and looking out the window, I couldn't tell anything and I certainly wasn't going to turn and give her a good once-over. She'd probably slap me just for looking.

A couple miles down the street, I turned my neck to check on traffic and saw that Ashley had freed Tom's cock from his trousers. One of her palms cupped his balls while the fingers of her other hand gently toyed with his shaft and tip. At least that's what I assumed, since I certainly wasn't looking closely. Okay. So I looked. I watched. I tried to pretend it wasn't Tom.

Alice spread her legs, exposing a reflective flash from her pink panties.

Soon after, Ashley was softly moaning and I guessed that Tom had snuck a few of his fingers beneath her skirt and between her legs. I concentrated on driving, as best I could, but couldn't help it as my own cock hardened and pressed against my jeans.

I'd never been so close to people who were having sex before. Not unless you count through the wall of a motel room. I could only imagine what was happening in the backseat. It was rare that I actually had the chance to glimpse back and see what was happening. The next time I did, as we were merging to the right, I thought that Ashley had somehow vanished, only to see that she'd bent down so her lips and tongue could work their magic on Tom's cock.

All the while, my date, Carol, still was sitting quietly, staring out her side window.

As we got ever nearer to Carol's house, I tried to think of excuses I could use to make the trip last longer. What was happening in back was so hot that if I hadn't had to concentrate on the road, I would have jerked off right there onto the steering wheel.

Then, I noticed something. Well, a couple things.

While trying to spy traffic in the passenger's side mirror, I noticed that it had moved and I couldn't see the traffic behind us very well. Then I saw why it was moved. Carol had a better view of what was going on in the backseat than I did.

Maybe my blind date wasn't as cold as a tray of ice cubes after all.

I became more curious about what was happening with the woman beside me than with what was going on behind me. And that's when I saw that Carol's right hand had disappeared beneath her trench coat.

If I'd been horny before, I was a lot more now. Instead of finding excuses to look backward, I kept one eye on the road and the other on my date.

She was subtle. As subtle as a person a couple feet away could be while they were masturbating. Since they were still covered by her trench coat, I could barely tell that her legs were parted. And though her legs hardly moved, I did see her toes bending and gripping inside her shoes. Pretty soon, her right arm started to shudder with a sexual rhythm that matched the humming of the car's engine.

The farther we drove, the faster her arm rocked. I could even hear short wisps of air escaping from between her lips as her shoulders relaxed and her legs instinctively shifted wider apart. Suddenly, and not more than a few miles from our destination, Carol snapped out of her little trance and, blushing, slowly swiveled her eyes to look at me through her glasses.

Carol hadn't treated me very well that evening. She'd dressed as though expecting torrential rains and she'd made me feel as welcome as an unexpected bill.

Still, I couldn't help but act the gentleman.

"Don't worry about it," I said. "If I weren't driving, I'd be doing the same thing."

Immediately, Carol smiled. First time since I'd met her. It completely transformed her face. She was stunning. I cannot believe I hadn't noticed how perfect her cheekbones were or that her eyes were an emerald green or that her lips were naturally plump and moist. It was as I was noticing all this and finding that I was as aroused by her as by what was going on in the backseat that she leaned across her seat, kissed my neck, and whispered, "We're almost to my place. If you can hold on until then, maybe we can take care of each other."

As she said, it was just another couple turns and we were in her driveway. I looked to the house, and imagined how fast we could make a mess out of her bedsheets.

"Should we go inside?" I asked. Actually, it was more like begging.

"I can't wait," she whispered as she kicked off her shoes and tugged free of her seat belt. She slung her coat off her shoulder and then tore apart her shirt, flashing her subtle breasts and large nipples at me. "On top of that, I like the car."

I was a little surprised but ready to go along. If she liked the car, then I loved it. On top of that, I couldn't wait either. If the steering wheel hadn't slowed me down, I'd have been on top of her before she had time to blink.

On my way to Carol I noticed that the mood had changed in the backseat. There were no more giggles. No quiet embraces or stolen kisses. Our companions were sitting on opposite sides of the car and staring away from one another. I was too occupied to worry very much about it. Though, I suspected, and being best buds with Tom, I more than suspected, that one of them had come too quickly and the other, not at all.

Carol's ass scooted across the seat under me as I wiggled my pants below my knees. Her back arched up and her neck thrust forward, allowing my lips to lock on to hers. Her legs spread as her insoles scraped my legs, forcing my pants to wrap down to my ankles.

"Oh," she suddenly gasped as her glasses popped off her face. "Is that you?"

"No, it's the emergency brake. Move left," I explained.

She shifted to the side, and spread her legs wide, her knees resting against the back of the seat and the dashboard. I ignored the cramps that were building in my thighs and buried my face in her neck, licking from the base upward until my lips wrapped around her earlobe. She sighed as her hands slapped at my hips, begging me to move forward. She was so wet that my cock slipped inside her easily, though I felt every millimeter of her tightness. Surprised at my speed, her eyes rolled back as a thin, red blotch spread across her upper chest.

She'd slap my ass, I'd thrust, she'd moan. Slap, thrust, moan. Over and over. The beat quickening as the veins on my neck were popping. I tried to hold myself in as long as I could. Only once was the rhythm interrupted. Once, when her palms cupped my cheeks and she looked into my eyes and whispered, "Jack. Oh, Jack."

She'd been paying attention that evening. Until then, I'd have bet against her even knowing my name. Those simple words were enough for me to lose control. My mind went animal, forgetting to worry about anything. I thrust as deep as I could reach into her, pumping like a shocked garden hose. Drawing back, I slipped out, and a stream puddled in her neatly trimmed pubic hair. Her eyes and lips widened, missing me in her, then rounded in delight as I entered again, and again. And again.

Our cries mixed. I didn't even care that our company had inched up and were peeking over the front seats at us.

As our breaths calmed, I rested my weight on her, nibbling her neck and earlobes with, already, renewing desire.

"I'd like to go home." Ashley's frosty words came from behind us, breaking the mood.

I whispered into Carol's ear, kidding, "Want to come along?"

"It's not a long enough trip, but how about getting together again? Maybe tomorrow night?" She sat up quickly, and I almost fell to the floor. "You know. Nothing special. Maybe we could just go for . . ." she paused before continuing.

"Another ride."

"Another ride?" I thought. What a perfect idea.

"But this time," the words poked through her mischievous smile. "I'll drive."

Ellie Naylor

JennaTip #4: Sex in Cars

First, this tip will begin with a real-life warning for those who intend to have sex in a moving vehicle. In September 2007, a twenty-two-year-old carnival worker was fined $188 in Idaho for leaving the scene of an accident after wrecking his SUV into a telephone pole. His excuse was that he lost control of his already top-heavy vehicle because two acquaintances were having what must have been very active sex in the backseat. They were lucky to only have minor injuries. The 22-year old had a $188 fine and had to pay for the repairs to his truck.

Now that you have been duly warned, the following are just a sampling of possible positions to try:

Front seat missionary position: The woman is in the fully reclined passenger seat. The man places his feet on the floorboards while facing her and positioning himself between her spread legs. The woman may either have her feet on the floorboards or on the dash. She can put them around his shoulders or against the roof, really, if she so desires. Go for it!

Front seat her on top: He is on the fully reclined passenger seat with her kneeling astride him for this position. Her being on top gives her control and the ability to more easily masturbate her clitoris manually or by grinding against his pubic bone. Be careful not to accidentally release the parking brake in this position.

Backseat 69: The woman is on her back with her legs spread while the man hovers above her on his hands and knees facing her feet. She can use her hands and mouth to manipulate his cock while he can use his mouth and tongue to lick and suck on her labia, clitoris, and insert his tongue into her vagina. Basically, yes, it's a 69 in a car.

Front seat driver's seat: Move the seat as far back as possible and adjust the steering column for additional legroom. While he is seated on the bottom and able to operate the gas, break, and clutch, she is seated, perched on his cock and is operating the steering wheel and the shift as needed. This is not safe and don't do this in highly trafficked areas if you insist upon actually having sex while driving. This can also be performed with her kneeling to either side of the man's thigh and facing him, but then it is up to him to do the driving. This may not be so comfortable. A story that's been passed along is of a woman who did this on I-95 going down to Florida with her boyfriend to scuba dive and had massive bruises all up and down her shin from the hand brake.

Front seat blow job: He drives and she leans over, putting her wet lips around his engorged cock. She bobs up and down and licks and sucks him until he comes. This can be done with both partners keeping their seatbelts in place and it is less likely to cause other people to wreck trying to figure out why some half-naked woman is sitting on some guy's lap, bouncing up and down and steering her car all over the place. It is likely to get a big honk and thumbs-up from passing truckers, however.

Beating the Heat

Misty was working the pole, curling her naked limbs around it like a lover. Big and blond, Misty is a nice Southern gal with a wide smile and wider ass who dreamed of being a real showgirl. In the meantime, she had to make do with a not-so-swanky club in the shadows of the big Vegas lights.

She was finishing up, unsnapping her top and shaking her tits at the near-empty room, when I heard a loud pop near the main stage. The noise caused Misty to jump, shaking her tits and ass even more aggressively. The lights flickered, and then the air switched off. Immediately the club became stuffy and smelled like feet. Some famous French guy once said: "hell is other people." He didn't know what he was talking about. Hell is working in Vegas on the hottest day of the year in a strip club with no air.

Jade stalked toward me, flipping her long, brown braids over her shoulder. She had a scowl on her face and a swagger to her steps. At almost six foot, she was built like an Amazon, all tits and muscle.

"How the fuck we supposed to work in this heat?" she spat.

I shrugged. I'm just the guy in charge of the music and lights. I pointed at Greg, our main bouncer. "Talk to him. The boss said he's in charge until he gets back."

"And when's that?"

"Beats me," I snapped back. "I'm no secretary."

Jade smirked, not saying anything more. I studied the way her ass swayed as she made her way toward Greg. She caught me watching and threw me a wink. Sometimes she took a mean turn, but generally she was okay, sweet even.

She didn't have the diva attitude like Misty, who'd left the stage and pretended to be gliding over rose petals on her way over to me.

"What happened to the air conditioner?" she asked, her arms pushing her D-cups together.

"Went out's my guess." Sarcasm was wasted on her but it didn't stop me trying.

Misty's face breathed into mine as she pushed out her bottom lip. It was supposed to be a pout but looked more like a grimace. "Do you still expect us to work? It's fucking hot!"

I shrugged. Besides the staff, the only other body in the place was some guy in the corner. He had a salt-and-pepper beard that looked older than his thirty-something years and wore a grayish plaid flat cap that was four decades out of style. His dress shirt, so blue it made my eyes water, had more wrinkles than a damp palm. Although his bouncing eyes seemed to be watching everything, he didn't seem to give a shit about anything other than the diet sodas he'd been nursing all afternoon. I bet myself he wouldn't even tip anyone.

"Not that I really give a shit, Misty, but why don't you offer that guy a lap dance if you don't want to work the stage?" She hated giving lap dances. Never wanted to be that close to the client.

"Fuck off," her words were deadpan and spoken behind her as she bounced toward the dressing room. I could have told her that it'd be hotter in there than out in the main area. But I'd let her find out on her own.

"Where's the damn music, Mr. Deejay?" That was Chloe. At barely five feet, her mouth was bigger than the rest of her. Black hair with wicked green eyes, while she wasn't as busty as some of the other girls, she was a dynamo on the dance floor.

She approached the stage and threw a CD at me. "Put this on. I'm sick of hip-hop."

I popped the CD in. "You still planning to dance?"

"Why not? A little sweat never hurt me." She shook her perky tits at me before performing a dainty pirouette and heading for the stage. She was right. Sweat never did hurt a girl.

I saw the hostess and one of the new dancers leaving. I didn't blame them. My T-shirt was already wet, and the air just kept getting thicker.

I dimmed the lights until I saw Chloe throw me the finger. As usual, she wanted the spotlight, air or no air. My fault. Long ago I'd pointed out that the spotlight highlighted her toned arms and tight gut. What Chloe wants, Chloe gets.

I expected music with a booming bass, but her choice was more understated, a melodic ambient tune with a gentle beat. Bedroom music.

She strutted down the stage in her signature black leather bikini. She didn't need an elaborate costume, just the switch in her hips and the fire in her eyes. For the next few minutes, she owned that stage.

The muggy temperature actually suited the music. Instead of the usual heavy grinding, her movements were serpentine as she swayed her hips like a kinky hula dancer. She peeled her top off, grazing her fingertips over her natural B-cups. The other girls thought she should go a size bigger, but personally, I approved her handfuls. They seemed just right.

Running her fingertips through her hair, she slid down the stage toward the pole. Embracing it, she climbed like an acrobat. When she reached the top, she gripped it with her inner thighs. No hands. Using only her leg muscles to slowly slide to-

wards the floor. About midway, she paused to do a half-crunch.
Twisted slightly to show off her lean upper body. She extended
her hands behind her head and slid all the way to the floor.
Arching her back, she rolled around the stage like a cat.

All this was done in perfect time to the slow music.

For the first time, her only real customer showed some life.
First, he tossed his cap onto the small table next to him. Then he
leaned forward in his chair to rest his hands on his knees. He
wiped the sweat off his forehead. I don't know if it was from
Chloe's routine or from the thick, muggy air in the club, but
was willing to guess it was both.

Jade glared at the guy, then called for Misty. They suddenly
seemed determined to get a tip off him. Misty hates working the
customer, but she hates the idea of Chloe getting his attention
when she couldn't. The pair positioned themselves right in front
of their audience of one.

Neither normally went for joint shows, so I was curious. By
the time I'd found a spot with a sweet view, they were topless
and kissing. Jade's back was shiny with oil and sweat, showing
off her defined muscles.

I glanced at the guy. He didn't seem interested in the action
in front of him. No. With a faint smile on his face he was peering
around them at Chloe. Boy, they were going to be hell on
wheels later. But Chloe could hold her own and I didn't worry.
She sure could hold his attention, which got mine back, too.

Onstage, Chloe was on her back, calmly stretching her legs
towards the ceiling while twirling her thong on one finger. She
shifted her legs, giving us all a good look at her bare pussy.

It was hard to take my eyes off Chloe, but the temptation to
check on Misty and Jade was mighty strong. Misty was kneeling
on the floor, tugging Jade's G-string down to the knees. Then,
she slid up the Amazon's lean body, pausing to stick her tongue

in her navel. It was the first time I heard Jade giggle. Misty continued upward, until the two were kissing, lightly at first like a brushing of smiles, then with deep tongues as their arms wrapped around each other.

I rubbed sweat out of my eyes. Jade was nodding her head to the beat as she and Misty, glistening with sweat and more, writhed against one another. Misty's hand dropped between them, finding Jade's clit with her long fingers. I wanted to keep watching but out of the corner of my eye I caught Chloe hopping down off the stage.

Dancing in short steps and an occasional full twirl, she moved toward the guy who'd been so interested in her. In response, his back straightened.

When near, Chloe spun half round, then perched her ass on his lap. Pressing her flat palms against her chin, she looked down with wide, wild eyes as her body shook sharply from side to side.

I'd seen her do that every time she sat on a customer's hard-on, and I never got tired of it.

It seemed that Chloe had decided to up the ante in this little competition. Jade and Misty didn't have a chance, but that wasn't going to stop them. They were clearly having too much fun. After all, it was just a little friendly contest to see who could squeak some kind of tip out of the guy. It's Vegas, after all.

Chloe stood, turned around, and touched the floor with her hands, giving him a long look at her tight ass. She circled his chair, pausing to shake her breasts right in his face.

Misty and Jade decided to take a break. Their bosoms heaved as they tried to catch their breaths. Everyone focused on Chloe as she straddled the guy's lap, squeezing his thigh with hers.

Chloe shook her hair out of her face and ground her ass hard into him. She threw her head back, her hands holding onto the chair. She didn't feel the muggy air. She didn't care that we were all watching her. She was feeling the music, riding the vibe. Doing what she does best.

She pulled herself up until she was almost pressed against his chest. With a teasing leer on her face, she hooked a hand behind his neck. Brought his face against her breasts and rubbed her nipples against his lips. Just a taste until she pushed his face back. She leaned forward to press her clit against his crotch. Undulating her body, rubbing his hard-on until his head fell back against the chair.

Chloe rode him like she was fucking him hard. Bouncing on his lap, rubbing her ass into him. He shuddered with a quiet groan as his body tensed, then relaxed.

Chloe stood and untucked his shirt to hide the damp spot on his crotch. I had to give him credit. He lasted a lot longer than I would have.

Suddenly, the AC cranked back on and everyone sighed with relief. A few ripe customers wandered in, college guys. At about the same time, I saw the victim of Chloe's lap dance race out. He must have had his fill of naked women and diet sodas.

Chloe pranced over to me, so excited that her body trembled. "He tipped me!"

She held a business card with both her hands. No cash? Big deal.

"Look who it is!" She pushed the card in my face. I recognized the name, one of the biggest in video porn.

"He wants to hire me." She crossed her arms behind her back and stood on her toe tips.

"Wow, impressive," I admitted. "You'd probably make more in a week with him than a month in this joint."

"Sure would!" Her giggle turned into a laugh.

"You'd get health insurance, your own Web site, a fan club." It sure sounded tempting.

"Lots of days off, too." She was bragging now. "And I'd move to LA. Out of this desert. Near the ocean."

I handed the card back to her. "So, you going to take it?"

Chloe thought for a few moments, almost too many. Then she twisted away from me and fell back, and into my arms. Grabbing my ears, she pulled me in for a quick kiss before she spoke again.

"Nah, I won't take the job," she smiled. "I'm staying here. Got to keep my eye on my husband."

We kissed again.

Leigh Malone

I really sort of wanted him to be eaten by the sharks.

A Change of Circumstances

Sometimes it seems like everyone in Florida owns a boat. Some people use their craft for deep-sea fishing or diving. Some as status symbols—side-lawn decorations next to their pink flamingoes. Some for sightseeing. Others just seem to tow them around, back and forth on the highways.

Me? I use my twenty-two-footer to get the hell away from all those people.

Sure, I have friends and can get along fine with people I work with, but eventually everyone seems caught up with bullshit. I need time away from all the fake drama to stay sane.

I generally steer straight away from the marina, heading out to open ocean where I won't see another boat and the beaches are just a long, tiny blur. Out there, there are no sirens or traffic sounds, no idiots on their cell phones, and no one knocking on my door to sell me something. Look, I like kids. But I'm not buying any more magazines or chocolates to help them go to college. If I wanted to pay for a kid to go to college, I would get married and have one of my own. OK. So, I am bit of a bitch sometimes. When I get like that, that's when I get away. I get out by myself and hit the reset button on my attitude.

Then it's just me and the clean, salty air and the waves gently licking the sides of my craft.

And the waves licking my craft always soothes me, if you get my drift. Hitting my reset button is as much a mental thing as a physical one.

Then the last time I went, things played out a little differently.

I got out to my open sea, to my refuge, and I took off my bikini top and shorts before lying down on the deck's lounge chair to soak up some sun. I'm an intense kind of person and relaxing comes hard for me. Generally, I spend my time working out, running, and basically working off my nervous energy. All those hours pay high dividends by giving me a nice flat tummy, a slim but muscled body, firm thighs, shapely calves, and a tight butt.

I set my alarm clock, as I have been known to relax myself into a deep sleep for hours. Then I really coated myself with sunscreen. Massaging it into my arms and legs, my hips, my stomach, my breasts, and particularly my nipples. I burned myself there once and will never, ever burn there again. Plus rubbing and massaging my body is what helps me relax, that and the sun beating down on me, sweating out all the toxins of city living.

I finally dabbed some sunscreen on my newly waxed and totally hairless mound. My skin was soft and the lotion was slick, then I was getting slick as my fingers dipped and dabbled about.

I wasn't serious, however, and soon closed my eyes and just let my mind drift, not unlike the boat. It seemed like no time at all when, as I enjoyed the sway of the boat rocking on the ocean, I thought I heard a voice.

"Hello?"

A stowaway? I got up and glanced around the boat. No one. But when I looked over the side, I saw him. There, in the middle of nowhere, was a young man bobbing in the water like a buoy. He waved at me before sinking beneath the surface. Within seconds, he popped up again.

"What the hell are you doing out there?" I asked.

"It's a long story. One I'd love to tell you, but since I wasn't planning to be in the water and these waters have sharks in them, and I'm not the greatest swimmer, I'd prefer to tell it to you under different circumstances." He looked around a bit nervously before smiling up at me disingenuously.

"What different circumstances?" I asked. He had the golden brown tan that was common in Florida and from what I could see as he bobbed about in the water, he had a lean body with broad shoulders. His longish blond hair made me think he was a surfer who took a wrong turn and lost his board.

"Like, with me out of the water."

He seemed harmless enough, but I was all alone out in the middle of nowhere. Before I put down my ladder I asked a few more questions. Dumb ones, I realized as they came out of my mouth.

"Are you alone?" See what I mean.

He looked around.

"Just me and the sharks!" he proclaimed as he wiped salt water away from his eyes.

"It's pretty dangerous out here. Why'd you swim so far? It's much too far to swim back."

His eyes scanned the nearest land. "I didn't swim. I'm not a great swimmer. And you're right. It certainly is too far to swim back."

"I suppose I should invite you onboard." I thought about turning the engine on and finding a different spot. But that would have been cruel. I may be a bitch at times, but I'm not quite that vicious.

"That'd be nice of you. I'd certainly appreciate it."

"You aren't some kind of deranged serial killer, are you?" As if he'd admit to it if he were.

"Nope. Definitely not." He seemed honest enough.

So, I tossed over the ladder and lent him a hand coming aboard.

"Well, now that you're aboard, I suppose I'm stuck with you."

It was only as he pulled himself up and over the side that I noticed he wasn't wearing a bathing suit. He wasn't wearing anything, actually. I was beginning to think I'd made a strategic error in allowing him up. I thought of pushing him back off, but since he was totally nude, I knew he wasn't armed, at least not with a weapon, well, at least not a weapon that wasn't attractively swaying between his legs in full view and not looking dangerous so much as looking *dangerous*.

He was on the deck a moment later. He was taller than I expected, maybe close to 6'3" with long legs and a firm torso. His golden tan extended all over his muscular body.

This guy wasn't just tall; he was damn long as well. And it was growing as his eyes wandered from mine and down across my body. Oops. In the excitement, I'd forgotten I was greased up and completely nude as well. I looked around for a towel, a blanket, or an evening gown.

"Sorry. It's the most honest part of a man's body." He didn't try to hide his hardening cock. No drama with this guy. He was, pardon the pun, "up front" with his desires.

I knew why I wasn't wearing anything, but for the life of me could not come up with a reasonable explanation for why he wasn't or why he was where he was.

"You were going to tell me that long story." I barely could say the word "long" without staring at his really lovely cock.

"How about I tell you under different circumstances?" Again with the avoidance.

"What circumstances would that be?"

"After I'm not so distracted." He licked his lips and damn if his tongue wasn't awfully, wonderfully long as well.

I stopped looking for cover and watched as he grew fully erect. I couldn't deny that I was aroused and having a hard time staying focused on the conversation, too. I also assumed I was either asleep and dreaming because I just couldn't get my head around this situation. I mean, really, where had he come from? Why was he naked? Also, if I was asleep, then doing what I knew I was about to do wouldn't be anything more than my subconscious having its way with me.

Sensing my desire, he smiled.

"When in Rome . . . or on a boat with a naked woman . . ." He murmured.

I stepped toward him, my hand dropping below to touch the soft hairs surrounding his huge erection. I stroked him lightly, enjoying how he filled my hand. I slid my palm over his head, softly massaging him until he groaned.

With his mouth buried in my neck, he gently pushed me back onto the deck, his warm body covering mine.

Without so much as a pause for a quick check, he entered me. Good thing I was already wet and willing.

In slow motion, one hard inch after another, he worked his cock into me. Using my own personal lubricant, he was slowly able to stretch me wider, until he was completely inside. After that, his first few strokes were careful, as he hit me in all the right places.

I wrapped my legs around his waist and clung to his muscular back. I was unable to close my wide-open mouth; short huffs escaped my throat every time his cock moved and I wiggled my hips in time.

Without warning, he grabbed me by the waist and rolled. One fluid motion until his back was on the deck and I was on top. I leaned forward with my hands on his powerful chest as I rode him fast and hard. I slid up that long, veined cock, then down again, grinding against him, smashing my mound and clit and then I'd push back up, coming down again hard.

He tried to get his thumb between us to press and rotate

against my sweet clit, but I was doing a good enough job grinding it up against him that he gave up and grabbed my hips to guide me up and pull me down.

Pretty soon, I was soaked with sweat, my hair hanging in my eyes, and I could feel the heat beginning. My stomach muscles started to clench and I was having difficulty breathing. My neck felt warmer and then warmer still as the blood started to rush. My scalp tickled and tingled and my toes began to curl. I closed my eyes and tried hard to breathe through it, but ended up holding my breath until it started escaping through my clenched teeth like a whistle almost at first until it turned into an outright scream and I threw my head back and dug my fingers into his chest. He groaned and came as I collapsed on top of him in a slick, trembling mess. I don't know how long I lay like that. Exhausted and giddy, I rolled off him and lay on my back, panting.

Suddenly, an annoying buzz blasted into my ear. I got an instant headache as my eyes snapped open. The late afternoon sun blinded me as I snapped off the alarm clock. I reached for my lover. But all my arms grabbed were ocean air.

He was gone. I looked over the side, searching for his blond hair or shark fins. Nothing there that I could see. I searched the boat. No one was there.

He arrived out of nowhere and now seemed to have vanished back to nowhere. While I had assumed I was dreaming, I just knew that I wasn't. It was too real. It was too good. I have sex dreams, of course, and even sometimes orgasm in my sleep, but not like this, not this vividly. But there was nothing to say he'd really been there.

Nothing except the note I finally saw fluttering in the light breeze and held down by what had at one point been my life preserver and rescue raft with a small outboard and was now one big empty space.

"Borrowed a few items. Didn't wish to disturb your sleep. By the way, you're incredibly sexy when you snore. Wish I could have stayed. Under different circumstances, I'd love to tell you the story."

Now, when I'm out on my boat, I'm just waiting for my circumstances to change.

Cory Walters

JennaTip #5: Being the Woman on Top

The entire JennaTales series is called *Erotica for the Woman on Top*. Well, there are reasons.

1. Jenna is definitely on top of her game. She's a powerful businesswoman, a cultural icon, the very definition of sex and sexy.
2. Because being on top in sex or being the top in an S&M relationship means being in control, being the decision maker, being the one calling all the shots. There is something to be said for being the Woman on Top and this tip says it all.

It's a favorite position for women for many reasons. It's also a guy's favorite. He gets to relax, be the one receiving attention, and he has an amazing view, which is very arousing for the majority of men. For her, she controls the angle, the depth, the speed, the rhythm. She can better stimulate her clitoris with her own hand, against his pubic bone, or he can better stimulate it for her with his fingers. The right angle can also help him hit the G-spot, something that almost never happens (unless he has a really curved cock—see Sex Tip: Bent Penis) in basic missionary-style sex.

There are several variations of the position and you should try them all and find the ones you love, the ones that help you reach the TOP and topple over, the ones you get wet over just imagining them with the hot delivery boy while languishing during boring work meetings.

Choose liberally from this sampling:

1. Man on his back, woman on top leaning forward resting her hands on the bed next to his head. This allows for kissing, tickling him with hair, brushing his chest with breasts and nipples.

2. Man on his back, woman facing away either sitting upright or leaning forward gripping his ankles or resting hands on the bed. This gives him a great view of his cock entering her and also gives him easy access to her anus for touching, caressing, and fingering. This position is commonly known as the "Reverse Cowgirl."

3. Man is sitting with his legs spread wide, woman faces him sitting on his thighs with her arms and legs wrapped around him. This is very much like an embrace.

4. Man is sitting, woman sits on his lap facing away. She can lean over to touch the ground giving him a different angle of access and view, bounce up and down on his cock while sitting upright. She can lean back into him, he can put his hands on her hips to guide her up and down, reach around to her breasts, and also reach around to her clitoris.

5. Man lies on his back, woman lies on him with her legs along his body. His legs are generally shut. This can be very good clitoral stimulation for her as she grinds hard against his pubic bone.

6. Man is sitting with his legs spread wide, woman lies on her back with her legs around his waist, resting on her elbows and looking back up at him. This provides a different angle of entry.

She sounds like a big, wet, red berry just bursting with juice begging to be bitten and squeezed and dipped in cream . . . ummm.

East Meets West

I'd always sworn I'd never haul my rig cross-country over a long weekend break. But, here it was, late Monday afternoon nearing California's border. I was barely getting through it, what with all the holiday traffic, the lousy drivers cutting me off, and seeing as I was all worked up from listening to Playboy Radio for the last five hundred miles. I'd tuned in to listen to a call-in show and got caught up in it and now here I was just hitting the California line, horny as hell, and not likely to be getting any relief anytime soon.

If it hadn't been my best client begging me to do this, and offering me a nice tip in exchange, I never would have agreed. In twenty-eight years, I'd been to thirty-one states, but had planned on skipping California for this lifetime. Nope. This Georgia girl didn't need any of that Hollywood sizzle. From what I seen in the movies, it'd take at least two of those starlets to equal my weight. Closest that ever came to being my size was that poor Anna Nicole gal and she starved and drugged herself to death, looking all crazy and sick. I love my round curves and so has every man I've been with, and I've been with my fair share. No one wants to be all bruised and poked to death by some skin and bones when fucking hard. At least that's what I found.

Nor did I need any of that famous southern California sunshine. Mind you, Georgia is a hot and sunny place, but we've got a big old canopy of oak trees for shade and while some people complain about the humidity, it keeps my skin plump and moist, just like the rest of me. Here I hadn't even dropped off this load yet and I already had my mind set on my backslide, my return trip.

Just before the border there were all kind of signs for trucks my size. And, having heard how mean and nasty, I mean alert and efficient, the California Highway Patrol can be, I followed them right along. Right toward what was called an Agricultural Checkpoint. Cripes. As if the world wasn't complex enough, California had to make things up to make it all even harder.

The line of trucks in front of me was long enough to promise an hour delay. I watched as the agricultural officers worked the other trucks. They had the driver open up the back. One inspector would go in and look around. Then, he'd hop down and close up the truck. His partner would have moved on to the second truck in line, doing the same. They were efficient enough that the line moved a lot faster than I thought it would.

Finally, one of those inspectors came up to my cab. He seemed to be my age, trim with wide shoulders and narrow hips and with a sweet little mustache. And he was browner than a paper grocery bag.

I hoped he knew English because I sure as hell didn't know any Spanish.

"Hello." He tipped his cap neatly. "How are you this afternoon?"

Well, hell. He spoke English better than me. And he was politer than me, too.

"Fine. But tired and in a rush. What's going on here?"

"We're looking for bugs." He figured that was all he had to say.

"Sweetie," I cooed. "No bugs in here. My truck is the cleanest one on either side of the Mississippi."

"I'm sure it is. But we have to check all incoming trucks.

California's economy is heavily dependent on its agriculture. Outside insects could cause us big problems." He was kind to explain. And I hadn't known that California had so many farms. I thought it was mostly concrete sidewalks and handprints.

"What are you carrying?" I knew he'd ask. Every stop, every weigh station, they always asked that. And I really didn't want to answer, but I did.

"Condoms," I said.

"What?" He lost his crisp manner for a second.

"Condoms. You know, rubbers. For people and sex." He looked a little embarrassed, so I added with a whisper, "Don't worry, honey. I don't plan on using them all myself."

After that, he followed me around the back of the truck and had me unlock and swing up the back gate. It was then I saw that a lot of the boxes in the back had fallen off their pallets. Some were crushed. And condoms were scattered all around. It must have been from that damn speed bump in Colorado.

"Ma'am, are you absolutely sure this is the cleanest truck on both sides of the Mississippi?" He teased through a wide smile.

He had to inspect the inside, and I followed him, not being able to help but admire how tight and fit his ass looked through those uniformed slacks. We worked our way toward the back, avoiding condoms as best we could, until he was satisfied that my truck had no bad bugs.

Then, the damn back door swung closed, leaving us in darkness thicker than swamp mud. Of course, he had a flashlight. He clicked it on and it flickered for a second, then flashed off.

I froze, heard him step next to me. His thick forearm brushed against my breasts. "Grab my arm," he said.

I'm a sucker for nice forearms. I held on as he led the way toward the door. His bicep grazed my rack, but it wasn't his fault. My girls are more than a handful.

About halfway down the truck, I lost my footing. Slipped on some rubbers and fell facefirst. Now I'm not one of these size-zero LA girls. I've got some meat on my bones. So I was surprised when he caught me. Hooked his arm around my waist before I could fall. I was surprised and damn impressed.

"Nice catch, sugar."

"Not a problem."

I touched his strong arm and took a step forward. "Are you always such a gentleman?"

"Only to the pretty Southern belles."

It had been a while since a man made me blush. "Aren't you a sweetheart?" I meant to give him a peck on the lips. I missed. I kissed him on the neck, letting my lips linger.

He still had his arm around me, pulled me close. Close enough for me to know that he was a sucker for this Southern gal.

"Dangerous weapon you have there." I dropped my hand and squeezed his hard-on. He responded by sticking his tongue in my mouth. I like a man who knows how to really kiss a woman. By the time we paused, my panties were already damp.

He gently pushed me down to the floor, raised my shirt, and unhooked my bra. Free, my breasts sprung out like they needed a breath of air. He couldn't help but grab onto them as his mouth moved everywhere, between my breasts, on my nipples, down my stomach, lower. He tugged my boots off one by one. Tossed them out of the way. His mustache tickled me in all the right places as he undid my jeans and peeled them toward my ankles. He did the same with my panties, only slower. By the time they reached my feet they must have looked like a knotted rope.

He spread my legs for me, helping to hook my heels on the edges of wooden pallets. Then his tongue and mustache began teasing my calves. Alternating between left and right and back again. Moving towards my thighs. I invited him further with a soft moan and his lips moved between my thighs as his tongue slowly circled my slit.

He used a finger, or maybe a thumb, to penetrate and press down as his mouth made my ass and hips grind against his face. And just in case he had any ideas about stopping, my palms grabbed onto his ears and held him right there. Right where I wanted him. And he put the hammer down.

It was just a tingle at first and I wasn't even sure I was coming. But the feeling grew fast and soon I was begging him not to stop as my legs wrapped tight against his neck. Oh, he was a real man, all right. Through all my bucking and grabbing and yelping he didn't take his aim off his target once.

Still breathing hard, I grabbed the closest handful of condoms and wagged them at him. "I don't know what you like, but you can take your pick."

He didn't even have time to take off his pants. Just pushed them past his muscular thighs and rolled on a condom. I had the urge to suck on his thick hard-on. He had other plans. He draped my ankles beside his neck and used his shoulders to push my legs up. I had no idea I was that flexible. Then he slid into me faster than a yellow light turns red.

It was a hard fuck, just my style with a steady rhythm that I could follow. His strong arms close enough for me to turn my head and lick. He held it. Took his time. Making sure I came again.

Just when I thought he was finished, he stopped and pulled out. His thick arms flipped me over like I was lighter than a pillow. He propped my hips up, my ass high in the air. When he found the angle he liked, he slammed into me, hard enough to make me cry out. He held onto my hips with both hands and hit the same spot over and over. He fucked me like he was pissed at me. I loved every minute of it.

I knew he was close when he grabbed onto my long hair. Pulled my head all the way back as he thrust deep inside me. He came with a groan, collapsed onto my back. I was hot, sticky, but completely satisfied.

We were stepping outside soon after. He hopped down from the truck first and then took my hand and helped me. Not like I couldn't get myself off my own truck, but it was charming. We had an audience, too. All the trucks in front of us had moved on and a bunch more piled up behind us. We must have had that freshly fucked look because horns started wailing.

I blew him a kiss before I drove off. In return, he tipped his hat and winked, "Señorita . . ."

Maybe this California wasn't going to be so bad after all. I could take a few days off when this delivery was made and I figured I might just check out some of this state. But I promised myself that I'd stay away from that Hollywood place.

I didn't think people there were ready for me yet.

Stacey Newman

This would be the best diet ever. The only concern would be all the people who would waste away to nothing working hard to meet the next goal.

The F-Factor Diet

I'm in really great shape, normally, but after the twins were born I struggled to lose the last twelve pounds and it had been almost three years and the weight was still clinging to my hips and waist. I know that twelve pounds doesn't sound like that much, but I'm just a couple inches over five feet and that kind of weight is the equivalent of two dress sizes on my frame. On my husband, twelve extra pounds doesn't even make him loosen his belt because he's well over six feet tall with broad shoulders. I guess I'm just trying not to sound like I'm some spoiled little brat over the twelve pounds but I'll stop making excuses for myself and just get to the story.

Because I wasn't thrilled with the extra weight, I hadn't really gone and done any shopping in those three years, thinking that once I lost the last pounds, I'd treat myself to a real spree and buy lots of sexy outfits and lingerie but that until then I'd wear T-shirts and jeans and flannel.

My husband never complained, not once, about the weight. He told me that I looked wonderful. I just wasn't happy. I couldn't get back into my skinny jeans. I thought my boobs weren't as perky as before and, although my hubby insisted that he liked the extra meat on my hips because it gave him more to grab, I didn't.

And, because I wasn't happy about my body, I wasn't feeling sexy. It was definitely impacting the frequency of sex and also my pleasure. I felt so self-conscious, I couldn't seem to relax and let go and so I wasn't having orgasms as often, which meant I wasn't interested in sex as often. It's an ugly cycle to get on and harder than concrete to get off.

So, Nick, my husband, came up with a plan. He said he felt that I just didn't have the right motivation to lose the last pounds. His idea was that for every three pounds I lost, I would get a reward. He asked me to write out six or seven of my favorite fantasies and that he would choose from that list to create a reward incentive program for me for losing the weight. He's a sales trainer, so he's all about incentive programs and setting goals and things like that.

He decided to call this diet the F-Factor diet. He said the "F" stood for Fantasy, but I thought it really stood for "Fuck," as in me getting fucked. The first list I gave him was a little tongue in cheek where I put down that I fantasized about diamond earrings and a clean bathroom. He crumpled that list up and made me sit down and write a new one.

I struggled with it because it was hard to imagine living out these fantasies feeling like I did about my body, but he pointed out that I would be losing the weight, so I would be feeling better about myself and how I looked. He did have a point, so I sat down and thought about it.

My first fantasy was pretty detailed. In it, he undresses me carefully, focusing his attention on me entirely. He leads me to the bathroom where he has set up a white, rounded metal-back chair with a soft creamy silk cushion.

I sit and he fills a small china basin with warm, almost hot, water. The basin is curved along the edges with a rosebud pattern like the one my grandmother had on her nightstand.

Nick is wearing white cotton drawstring bottoms. They aren't quite pajama bottoms but are more like loose cabana-boy pants. He is barefoot and bare-chested. His dark hair is slicked back and he is clean shaven. He has on a chrome metal watch and his wedding ring. His skin glistens with oil, making his shoulder muscles ripple even more.

Nick has me spread my legs apart and then he uses a soft sponge to soak up some of the hot water. He drips it onto my furry mound, then wipes downward, squeezing to let out more water, as he applies it to my pussy. He gets the hair and lips and everything nice and wet. Then he takes a special, foamy soap and holds a scoop in his hand.

He gently applies the soap to one of my labia, massaging a little in small circles. His fingertips press into the flesh and push up against my clit. I am starting to breathe faster by now and my nipples are hard and erect.

Nick has this brand-new, sharp razor that is all pink and sexy looking, made of metal with a curved handle. He ever so carefully uses the razor to shave away the hair on my pink pussy, exposing my soft skin. Sometimes he slides the handle up into me, like a finger, so it taps against my G-spot. Sometimes, he blows lightly on my clit and I shiver from the cool air on my sensitive skin.

He applies more warm water and makes sure I am comfortable and relaxed. He is meticulous, removing small amounts of hair at a time and cleaning the razor on a dry, white cotton cloth.

He is kneeling there, between my legs and is so fascinated and concentrated on my beautiful flower, it is as though there is nothing else in the world. He shaves both sides baby smooth, leaving a triangle of hair pointing down to my clit.

Using warm oil, he drips and drizzles it onto my now clean and exposed pussy. He pours just a little on and massages it in, then pours more and massages it in until I am soft and glossy and smooth and pink down there. I, of course, have a mind-blowing orgasm just as he finishes his ministrations, heaving and throwing my head about. My nipples burn and my eyes are clamped shut as I cling to the metal chair, wracked with waves of pleasure. That's it. That's the fantasy. It ends here because fantasizing about the mind-blowing orgasm actually triggers my orgasm generally at just that same moment so I don't have to keep imagining. Also, I like this fantasy a lot because it is about me and about my pleasure and I don't even think about him doing anything but worshipping my sweet, wet spot.

The next fantasy I wrote out for Nick is one where we are out at a dark, busy club where I am leaning up against the bar wearing a short skirt without panties. It's really crowded with people pushing up to try to get their drink orders in and we're being jostled from all sides. Nick pushes up behind me in the crowd and slips his hands up under my skirt and massages my pussy lips and clit right there as I sip my drink and make idle chitchat with the bartender. I have to try to control myself as I orgasm, my pussy clamping around his thick forefinger.

Nick is wearing a long black leather coat and the way it hangs open it makes sort of a curtain around me, giving us privacy. Because of how many people are at the club and the loud music and the constant movement, Nick is pushed into me, again and again.

Finally, he leans me forward, and my tits are almost falling out of my top as I bend over resting my upper torso on the bar. He unzips his pants and then pulls out his raging hard cock. I am so wet from my orgasm that Nick easily slips it between my thighs and up into my waiting cunt. He fucks me, right there at the bar, and with the people still pressing forward and into us, it's like they are driving his purple helmeted cock into me to the rhythm of the music.

For the third fantasy, I wrote about being tied spread-eagled on our bed, naked, as Nick goes down on me, licking and sucking my cunt and clit. Nick oils my body, rubbing my tits and waist and hips and thighs. He licks me, sucking hard enough to bruise me, and darting his tongue in and out of me. He puts his hands under my ass cheeks and lifts my hips up so he can run his tongue from my clit to my ass and back. I cannot stop him, not that I want to, but he keeps going as I orgasm and orgasm and orgasm again until I faint.

I kept writing. Some were short fantasies, just ideas really, while others were really detailed. For example, I wrote about how I fantasize about him masturbating while sitting in the corner chair in our room. I am on the bed, just watching him. He has to take his time and really pleasure himself. I wrote about how it totally gets me off to watch as he pulls and rubs his cock. How I like for him to spit in his hand and rub his saliva along his long rod. How I like it when he cups his own balls with his other hand and pulls at them.

I described the beauty of his veined cock and how it makes me come to see him throw his head back and let out a guttural howl as the come shoots out all over his stomach and hands.

I wrote and wrote and wrote. I came up with, not six or seven fantasies, but like sixteen or seventeen. Just thinking about them and writing them down had me so hot and horny I thought I would die. I gave them to Nick, thinking he'd rip my clothes off me and fuck me right then and there, but you know what that jackass did? He said I had done a good job, he'd review them and come up with a plan, and that we would start on the reward program immediately.

I protested that I wanted to start rewarding myself and him right away, but he said that I had to lose my first three pounds before any fantasies or sex. God, what a self-controlled son of a bitch, but it worked like a charm. I lost those three pounds in just half a week. I'd been snacking between meals, eating choco-late, nibbling on things all day long. I simply cut out those snacks and drank lots of water and those first three pounds just melted right off me.

My first reward was the spread-eagle fantasy. But first, he had me read through the list he had made. He had only written down three of the sixteen I had given him. I understood that I was only planning to lose twelve pounds, but that would have been four fantasies but he said the last one for the last three pounds was going to be a surprise for me. He said that was a lit-tle bit extra incentive.

Reading through the list really got me going and horny again, so once I was tied down, he really didn't have to spend a lot of time licking and kissing and sucking my clit until I came. He pushed his fingers up into me and kept licking though. He mas-saged my ass and hips, he slid his thumb up into my ass, he reached up and pinched and tweaked my nipples and kept tongue-fucking me, and I really did have orgasm after orgasm until I was begging him to stop. I really did think I would have to faint for him to stop. He finally did stop with me still conscious, though barely, and I have to say that even though I was really tender, it was agony in the best possible sense.

The second three pounds took a little more effort. I started eating yogurt and granola for breakfast, I had chicken sand-wiches for lunch, and for dinner I would have half as much pasta as normal and a little salad. It took a full week to lose these three pounds, but I definitely was feeling a lot better.

My second reward was a shopping trip to the lingerie store where Nick picked out three amazing outfits for me. I had to put them on in the dressing room and walk out to model them in full view of any other shoppers. I had to do at least three full turns and count to one hundred in measured breaths before I could go back into the dressing room. I'm a total exhibitionist at heart, I guess, because this scared me but not nearly as much as it turned me on. I wanted to masturbate with the doorknob of the changing room I was so hot to go after I had showed off my first outfit.

It was a little pink baby-doll nightie with matching thong. It was sheer so my rosy areolae showed through. It was short, so my pink ass cheeks were in full view. I was extremely nervous but also excited and wet and hot as I thought of other random people seeing me in the lingerie. I saw several people stop and point or nudge friends. I didn't see anyone I knew. That was a relief, actually. I loved the idea of titillating strangers. I did not love the idea of shocking my twins' pre-school teacher.

The second outfit was a black lace demi-bra with matching garter, panties, and stockings. Nick even made sure I had some high-heeled slippers to put on with it. He also gave me a sheer black short robe but during the show he made me take it off and twirl in front of him just in the bra, panties, and stockings. I got some really appreciative looks from both guys and girls and felt absolutely sexy and amazing.

The last outfit was a pink and white corset with black laces and stitching. I cinched it in as tight as I could, put on the little bit of pink material they sold as a panty and stepped out to a crowd. I guess word had spread. I would have jumped back in, but the rules were the rules and I had to spin three times while counting to one hundred.

We bought all three outfits, of course. We slipped into the public bathroom at the department store after and I gave Nick a blow job in the stall. A few people came in while we were in there but we were really quiet. At least we tried to be really quiet. I sucked and licked his hard dick. He stood while I sat on the toilet. I deep throated him until tears came out of my eyes. He put his hands in my hair and fucked my mouth while I played with his balls. Then when he came, I sucked out all his come, licking my lips.

It was a great way to celebrate my halfway goal. I was feeling really great, super sexy, and hot. We would have been having lots of sex except he was refusing me any until I reached the full goal. I couldn't believe it, but he was so right, it did motivate me to keep going. I not only wanted to have my fantasy fulfilled, I wanted sex. If I had to lose three pounds to get it, then by damn, I was going to lose those three pounds.

I added in exercise to lose the next three pounds on my husband's F-Factor diet regimen. I was feeling and looking better after losing the first six, but didn't want to lose ground. I was also horny as hell and dying to have more of my fantasies come to life. While I hadn't been too interested in sex at first, having to come up with the fantasies jump-started my libido and then his refusing to have sex with me unless I lost the goal weight also kept me very motivated. He's a manipulative shithead, but I really couldn't complain because I was back to feeling like my old sexy self and I was losing the weight.

To lose the next three pounds and get some good, hot, lovin', I started walking every morning for twenty minutes. It didn't seem like much, but combined with my changed eating habits I met my next goal by the end of the week. I could not believe how much energy I had or how great I felt. My friends were noticing and commenting, too. I had a hard time not telling them and I grinned like the cat that ate the canary when I thought, *If they only knew the motivation.*

Well, my reward for those three pounds was really simple. Nick stayed late at work and at around eight p.m., I met him downstairs in the lobby of his building wearing a raincoat and nothing else. We went to the service elevator and called it to pick us up. It had a rubber mat on the floor, padded blankets hanging on the wall, and a utility cart with a bucket and cleaning supplies in the corner.

After the elevator started to climb, Nick hit the stop button and then lifted me up so I was sitting on the utility cart. He undid the tie of my coat, letting it fall open so I was sitting there before him naked and ready. He unzipped his fly, letting his hard cock flop out. I licked my hands and ran them over his rod, getting him all wet and superhard. Then he fucked me right there in the service elevator. It was quick and hard and dirty and I loved it. He just rammed into me again and again.

The cart wobbled and shook and I thought it would collapse entirely, but it held up. I grabbed the padded blankets next to me and behind me to get some purchase and ripped one of them right off the wall. The smell of cleaning supplies and the grunginess just added to the fantasy.

When we were done, we rode the rest of the way up, then packed up his things and went home. I would have loved to have had a second go up in his office, but I hadn't written it down as part of my fantasy, so he said no.

Even though I was frustrated, I was also turned on by his refusals.

I went to work on losing the last three pounds. It took a little more work and time. It was the holidays, so I gained a little bit of weight back, which meant I had to lose four pounds instead of three to get my final reward, but finally, after adding in an afternoon yoga class three days a week and cutting out the sandwich at lunch and replacing it with soup or salad, I lost those last pounds.

I had no idea what my final reward was going to be. I was so wound up and excited that when I weighed myself and saw that I had finally lost all twelve pounds, I screamed, waking Nick and scaring the hell out of him. He told me that the final fantasy was going to take a little more prep time. He told me that it would be fulfilled on Saturday night. It was Thursday morning and I wasn't sure I could wait, but he told me I would just have to.

Saturday morning came and went. Saturday afternoon came and went. The only thing not coming and going was me! I was distracted and kept forgetting things like where the keys were, that milk went in the refrigerator and not the cabinet, and what the kids' names were. At six p.m., Nick packed up the kids and took them to his mother's for the night. I paced up and down in the kitchen wondering what he was going to do.

The answer came when he got back forty-five minutes later. He opened the door and walked in the house, but he wasn't alone. Right behind him was Peter, his squash partner. Peter smiled at me and I blushed from my toes to my head and then turned pale as all that blood rushed to my pussy because I finally knew what the last reward was going to be.

Polite and soft-spoken, Peter looked good enough to eat, which was exactly my thought the first time we met. He was sweaty and wearing white shorts and a soaked T-shirt that clung to his chest. He and Nick had just had an hour-long bout and, as Nick's car was in for a tune-up, I had gone to pick him up. Peter's about the same size as Nick, but while Nick is dark, Peter is all sunshine with his sky-blue eyes and golden blond hair. We didn't really know one another well, as he was single and didn't tend to socialize in the same circles as my moms' group.

However, Peter had definitely made an impact on me and I did often picture myself sandwiched between my darling Nick and Peter. So, I had written about a fantasy I have that involves Nick and Peter when Nick asked me to make my list. I never in a thousand years thought that Nick would ever make this fantasy come true, but there stood Peter in my doorway on the ultimate fantasy night, the night I was celebrating having lost those final pounds and finally being able to fuck my husband good and regularly.

It was a little awkward at first, but after some talking and wine, we all started to relax and finally it was time to get going on the fantasy. I hadn't put in a lot of detail on this one because I was just too nervous about writing it down at all, so things were going to be fairly free form.

We were all in the living room, sitting on the couch, when Peter started to run his hands up my leg. Nick watched him do this, then leaned in to kiss me on my neck. Nick lifted a hand and placed it on my breast, squeezing it gently as his tongue continued to move up my neck to my ear. Meanwhile, Peter had adjusted so he was facing me, sitting sideways on the couch. He started to rub at his bulging crotch as he slid his hand up under my skirt. I was squirming around and not sure exactly who to concentrate on or what to do. I tentatively reached over and put my hand over Peter's and helped him rub his cock through his pants. Nick saw this, and slid his free hand up my skirt where Peter and Nick set about taking turns slipping fingers inside me and flicking at my clit.

It took only a few minutes and I came from the excitement and stimulation. As I caught my breath, Peter stood up and unzipped his pants. He pulled off his belt and slid the pants down and off. He then stepped out of his underwear.

I haven't looked at another man's cock in person in over eight years. It was amazing to see the difference. The color was lighter, he had curly golden blond hairs surrounding his shaft, the head was pink, not purple, and his balls weren't as dark either. It curved a little to the left. I was mesmerized. He brought his cock toward me and I was staring at it so attentively I almost went cross-eyed as the tip tapped against my lips.

I shook myself awake, parted my lips, and tasted his sweet skin. His pre-come was less salty than Nick's but there was more of it. I was so turned on by the sensation of trying something so new, I barely noticed that Nick had also stood and removed his clothes. Nick then sat back down and set about unbuttoning my top. He gently pulled it from my body, then undid my bra and removed it as well. Peter stripped off his shirt as I continued to let my tongue explore his hard cock.

With a little urging from Nick, I slid off the couch. Peter pulled out to let me get onto my hands and knees. He knelt in front of me, sliding his monster dick back into my mouth. Nick bent down and started to lick me from behind, inserting his tongue into my wet cunt. He licked up my taint to my puckerhole then back down again. I was getting really excited by having all this attention and came again as Nick thrust his tongue in and out of my pussy.

I started to pull and suck harder at Peter's cock, licking up and down the shaft and nibbling on the head. He started to moan and pulled out because he said he was going to come if I kept it up.

While he worked on relaxing so he wouldn't come too quickly, Nick slid his hard purple cock into me, pulling me up so I was upright on my knees in front of him. He massaged and fondled my breasts as he slid his dick in and out of me. Peter sat watching us, slowly rubbing his hard cock.

Peter soon had had enough sitting on the sidelines and he got off the couch and knelt in front of me. He started to play with my tits as Nick held my hips and kept pushing into me. Nick pulled his cock out of my cunt and slid it up between the cheeks of my ass. The head of his cock pushed and tapped at my asshole, which was slick from my come. Nick and I had tried anal sex a few times, but not very often. I was so hot and horny however, that when he popped it in this time, it felt fabulous and, again, I came.

With Nick's big cock in my ass, my pussy was available for Peter. Peter managed to slip his long hard rod up into me so that I was impaled on both men. It took some work to find the right rhythm, but we did. I was totally sandwiched between Peter and Nick, sweating and moaning, filled entirely with cockflesh. I couldn't believe that this was really me.

It didn't take long before I came again. As my pussy and ass tightened in waves both men also started to come. Nick pulled out and let the last of his ejaculate shoot onto my bare pink ass. Peter grabbed my hips and thrust hard into me, making sure that all his come went up into me.

Afterward, I realized what a sopping-wet mess I was, but right then I didn't care. I was so satisfied and exhausted, I just fell over and lay on the rug, my knees splayed out and arms flung up over my head. I barely remember Peter thanking Nick and me for the evening. I hardly recall Nick lifting me up and carrying me to bed. The incredible thing is I had the most erotic dreams that night and woke up crazy horny at about four a.m. I pounced on Nick, straddling him and pulling and manipulating his cock until he was hard, at which point I rode him until I had come twice.

Now that the F-Factor diet was over, I didn't have to wait until I had met my goal to get a good fucking and poor Nick didn't get a moment of rest for the next two weeks, as I jumped him at every opportunity.

My friends have all raved about the changes in me and begged me to tell them my secret. I just don't know if I'm ready to share the F-Factor diet plan with the world, although I bet it would be a best seller.

Adina Giordano

*Ooooh. Did you have a teacher just like this you used to
go to bed thinking really bad naughty things about?
I bet you did.*

Gaining Instruction

My old high school invited me to join its "Second Chance"
program. It was a program for people like me, people who,
through stupid mistakes, had failed a class and not earned their
degree. For a fee, alumni were being offered the opportunity to
return to school, retake the class, and receive their diploma as
long as they did the work and passed. I think it was mainly a
fund-raiser but I'd failed English and I shouldn't have. I had
good grades all through school but my last year, my last semes-
ter, my last paper I'd gotten a wild hair up my ass and decided
that I didn't have to play by the rules, those idiotic unwritten
rules about what a good, private school, school girl could write
about. It had always bugged me that I'd failed so unnecessarily.
So even while I owned my own very profitable and successful
catering business, I felt I had something to prove. Plus, I could
afford both the time and the money, so I signed up.

I had a few major concerns. How would a group of rowdy
and very competitive seventeen-year-olds take to having a woman
of twenty-nine in their class? Would they pick on me? What if
the teacher was some kid straight out of college? Could I respect
a teacher who was younger than me?

My fears were unjustified. Mr. Mansfield was a large, sternly
handsome man in his mid-forties. He didn't seem to believe in
detention and rarely had to raise his voice. Shocking considering
what my class had been like in high school and what I'd assumed
it had deteriorated to in the intervening years. He didn't punish

people because he never had to. A lift of his eyebrow silenced thirty chattering teens and a frown, one that wrinkled his brow, lowered his lids, and made his already solid jaw, granite, made hulking high school defensive linemen tremble. Half the girls, including me, had crushes on him.

So when, a week after I'd handed in my paper, I got a note telling me that Mr. Mansfield wanted to talk to me, I quaked. I was almost thirty, a successful businesswoman, and I didn't have to wear the school uniform, but I felt like a third-grader who'd been "sent to the office," with mud on my shirt.

I knocked on his door.

He said, "Come in."

I entered and sat in the chair opposite his desk. Mr. Mansfield looked at me with his craggy brow lifted. Grown woman or not, I was his student and I hadn't been invited to sit. I stood up, quickly, and put my hands behind my back. It was all I could do not to drop my eyes, toe his rug, and sway.

"Why did you fail English when you were at school?" he asked me.

"I got a bad grade on my final paper," I explained, feeling inadequate.

"Why?"

"Ms. Harper didn't like the subject I chose."

"How do you know she didn't like it?" I must have looked blank because he continued, "Did you choose it planning to fail?"

"Of course not," I protested.

"I've checked the records. You chose a topic about which you knew she had strong opinions. You elected to argue the alternative. While teachers should be able to set their personal feelings aside, they are only human. You knew her position. Why pick that topic?"

I bit my lip.

"Are you doing it again? Deliberately trying to fail?"

I tried to find words, but couldn't.

He frowned, paralyzing me. "Once more, you have chosen a politically incorrect position on a controversial subject. I repeat myself, which I despise doing. Did you want me to fail you?"

I shook my head.

He picked up a folder with my name on it. "You made no spelling or grammatical errors. As for your punctuation, you are overly fond of colons and semicolons, but I didn't deduct any marks for that. You made your argument passionately and well, except, it was entirely one-sided. What you should have done was describe the opposing arguments and demonstrate their flaws. You didn't do that, so I knocked marks off. You also argued from the specific to the general. You could have had a higher mark, but as it is, the best I can give you is a B-plus."

My legs almost gave way. He'd had me so sure I'd failed, and then he'd given me a much better mark than I expected. I squeaked, "Thank you, sir," and half-turned to go.

"I didn't dismiss you."

I swung back. "Sorry, sir."

"I will discuss the content of your paper with you, here, at three in the afternoon, on the twenty-third of this month. At that time, you will be instructed appropriately."

My mind spun. "But," I protested, "graduation is next week. I'll be finished. School will be out for the summer. I won't be your student anymore."

He looked at me and repeated, "Come for instruction at three, on the twenty-third."

I mumbled, "Yes, sir," and fled.

Of course, I didn't have to keep the appointment. He couldn't make me. He couldn't take my diploma back and I was free and an adult. Why would I even bother to return to an empty school and gain instruction from Mr. Mansfield? What did it matter if I argued from one side? Not much since, after all, I'd earned a B-plus, well above simply passing.

No matter what I said to myself, I knew I would go for instruction. I wanted to know what he really thought of my paper. It mattered.

There's a trunk in the crawlspace in my basement that I hadn't opened for ten years. In it, I found my old school uniform—the white shirt, the striped tie, and the gray flannel pleated skirt. I remembered us girls having to kneel upright in those skirts while our health teacher went round with a yardstick. The rule was that the hems had to be no more than a half inch off the floor, kneeling.

I tried my old uniform on, just to see if it still fit. It did, but the shirt needed washing and the skirt seemed shorter on me now than it had then. I found a pair of tassel loafers and a pair of over-the-knee thin cotton socks to finish out my look.

I told myself that by dressing up as a schoolgirl, I'd be making fun of my upcoming lecture from Mr. Mansfield—ridiculing the situation by exaggerating it. That's what I told myself. I almost believed it.

An empty school sounds hollow. The clicks of my heels echoed. There were butterflies in my tummy as I made my way through the corridors to Mr. Mansfield's office. What if my dressing up as a schoolgirl made him angry? I'd never seen him angry and I didn't think I wanted to do so now. I paused outside his door and took deep breaths, trying to decide whether to knock or to flee.

He said, "Come in."

One of his eyebrows twitched when he saw the way I was dressed but it didn't actually lift. I didn't make the mistake of sitting but stood with my hands behind me again, and this time I did drop my eyes and let my hips sway.

He got straight into his lecture. "You made a cogent argument about your topic. You explained clearly why you would benefit from structured discipline, enforced by corporal punishment," he said. "It is clear to me that you did your library research. I was impressed by what you learned about the chemistry of the brain, how measured pain produces endorphins, which can drug the subject into a state of euphoria. You reasoned that punishments such as spankings or canings can create bonds between the punisher and whoever is punished, which will make the subject eager to please, and I thought that was well done."

He paused and fixed me with his intense gaze. "You did not, however, cite any actual examples. While you have described the benefits of corporal punishment, you appear to have made your conclusions with no experimental evidence whatsoever. Why is that?"

I swallowed hard. "Um . . ."

"Were you spanked as a child?"

"No."

"Not by anyone? Father, mother, uncle, aunt, sibling?"

"Never."

"At school?"

"No."

"Have you ever experienced a 'recreational' spanking, from a lover, for example?"

"No."

"So your bottom has never been struck, not by a hand, nor a cane, nor strap, nor crop?"

I shook my head. "Never."

"Then how can you assert so vehemently that the experience would be both beneficial and pleasant?"

I pouted. "I just know. I've thought about it, a lot."

"Have you considered that the theory might be nothing like

the practice? How on earth can you take a firm stand on such a topic with zero experience?"

I repeated, "I just know."

"That's easy to say. Would you be willing to put your theory to the test?"

"Huh?"

"Don't grunt. I'm not telling you that you are wrong. What I am telling you is that you are not qualified to debate the issue until and unless you have been properly instructed in the matter. This is not a topic that you can make decisions about by pure reason. If you want to prove your point, you have to demonstrate it."

"Demonstrate?"

"By being caned, and enjoying the experience."

I squeezed my thighs together. It was obvious what he intended, but did I dare put my theory to the proof? "But who? When? Where?" I stammered.

He reached down behind his desk for an old-fashioned teacher's cane, three feet of whippy rattan with a curled handle. "Me. Now. Here," he said, and came around his desk with the fearsome weapon in his hand. "I intend to instruct you. I, if I say so myself, am fully qualified as an instructor in much more than English writing."

"I . . ."

"Stretch across my desk and get a good grip on the other side."

My mind numb, I obeyed.

"On the bare bottom, of course," he told me. I felt him lift my skirt's hem and tuck it into my waistband. "How many strokes to prove your point?" he asked. "A dozen, do you think?" His hand pushed my flimsy lace panties down to my knees.

I could hardly breathe. He'd bared my bottom and was looking at it. The shame of it made my cheeks burn. I managed to get, "Twenty-four, I think," out.

"That's ambitious, for your first time, but very well." The cane touched my thighs just above my socks. I felt it like a shock and trembled with fear and anticipation.

"I will administer the punishment in this area." The cane tapped the fullest part of my bottom. "Well?"

"Well?" I asked.

"You must ask for it, and properly."

"Please, sir, would you instruct me?"

"Yes."

The cane fell. I jerked. A line of fire burned across me, right on the crease where my bottom met my thighs. Another joined it, an inch higher. Tears started from my eyes. By the time he'd landed six strokes, I was ready to quit. All I was feeling was pain. I gritted my teeth and endured. At eight, a glow started to spread. By ten, the insides of my thighs were slick. There was still pain, and yet there wasn't. It still hurt, but it didn't. I was aware of the stinging and the throbbing but my mind was afloat in a sparkling mist. I entered a state of mental ecstasy. And I was vindicated. I was triumphant. I was fucking horny!

Mr. Mansfield, my beloved teacher, threw his cane aside. "That was twenty-four," he told me. "I'm proud of you." He paused. "Let me test whether you found the experience pleasant, as you argued."

He dipped a finger into my pooling cunt. I was soaked with sweat and desire from the exertion of being caned.

"You appear to have enjoyed it. Is that so?"

I nodded.

He slapped me lightly, but right on the hottest, reddest part of my bottom.

"Speak when spoken to, or are you in need of further instruction."

"Yes, sir."

"Be clearer. 'Yes, sir, I enjoyed it' or 'Yes, sir, I desire additional instruction'?"

"Yes, sir. Both, sir."

"Ahhh," I could hear the smile in his voice along with the rasp of his zipper being pulled down.

"Shall I instruct you now?"

"Yes, sir. Please, fuck me." I wasn't going to be unclear with him again.

My pussy was so wet and slippery that he slipped right in, filling me and distending me as no cock had filled me before.

He rocked gently, teasing me. "Your next course will be in creative writing," he said. "It'll be a private course, with your own personal teacher."

His rhythm accelerated.

"Will there," I asked, "will there be further instruction?"

"I can guarantee it."

"Then sign me up, sir."

Michael Clark

JennaTip #6: Oh! Spank Me, Part 1

How to spank your partner for ultimate results. Don't just start waling away at your lover and think you're going to get a wet, sexy, happy partner. A real spanking takes understanding, communication, agreement, and willing participants. With this in mind, the following is a guide to spanking for recreation.

1. ***Set the mood.*** Read a story that includes a good, hot, and sexy spanking scene. Watch a video with the same. Talk dirty to one another and get into role playing with spanking. Play pretend and dress up. Step out of your everyday roles and step into someone else's shoes. Tell your partner how bad they've been and why they deserve the spanking or tell them how sweet their ass looks or how once this is over you'll give them a very special treat. Have your partner tell you how it feels, cry, explain how sorry they are or be defiant and insist that no matter how much or how hard you spank them, they'll never change. Once you have the mood set, then start slowly and build up to the actual spanking. Lick the area, kiss it, rub and caress it before perhaps scratching it gently, then harder, or start with gentle taps that gradually progress to firmer slaps. Be creative.

2. ***Communicate.*** First you both need to be in agreement that spanking is what you want. It is very important that the "spanker" listen to and follow the feedback given by the "spankee." If you are a novice at spanking you probably don't know how hard or soft, where, how frequent, or how long without your partner telling you what they want. Even if you have spanked in the past, each person and each time is different. If you are too embarrased to talk about it, you aren't ready to do it.

3. **Be careful.** Aim for fleshy parts of the body such as the ass, thighs, and backs of the calves. Do not spank the back, particularly around the kidney area, as these are fragile and vital body parts that could be truly damaged.

4. **Be creative.** There are a variety of positions to explore when spanking someone. Be certain you have space to see where you are striking your partner and that you have control over the spanking. The most popular position is over both knees or scissored bent over one knee and held in place with the other leg holding down the spankee's legs. Your partner can also be on his or her hands and knees, ass in the air, or bent over a bed, chair, counter, car seat, table . . . use your imagination.

5. **Technically speaking.** This is a continuation of what we started talking about with setting the mood. Once you have progressed to spanking, then be sure to mix it up, spanking harshly and then gently, several quick slaps followed by a loving caress or kiss. Work at a steady rhythm of soft and slow to hard and fast but build up or you'll have a short spanking session from too much, too quickly.

6. **Hand spanking.** Your hand is more versatile than you may think and by using it you have the added enjoyment of feeling your partner's skin against your own. It is much more intimate to use your own hand than an inanimate object. Your hand also can be cupped or flat, you can scratch with nails or use the backside of the hand. In addition, don't just spank and don't just use your hand. Use your tongue, lips, breasts or balls, and breath to mix things up and add to the sensations.

7. **Finale.** Don't just abruptly stop. This is an emotional experience and it is important to have some closure. Count down to the last spank. This provides for a certain

amount of anticipation on their part and your part, too. Once the actual spanking is done, offer a nice massage or rubdown with oils or creams. If you broke the skin, which may happen with a prolonged spanking, use aloe vera or something else good for soothing scrapes and cuts. Be ready to cuddle after. It is as likely your partner will want to be held and stroked and perhaps have slow and gentle sex as have you plow a new row with hard sex.

I love the tabloid nature of this one, the dirty underbelly of Hollywood and the recognizable (but not too recognizable) characters.

Money Shot

I had to climb down a metal rainspout to get there because the ledge I was aiming for was a good twelve feet down from the apartment building's roof and a bad two feet wide. In the moonlight, the traffic below looked like burning matches. I'm not a fan of heights, but I'm less a fan of being evicted for nonpayment of rent, so if being up here was going to get me my rent money, and I hoped a significant bit more, then fear of heights be damned.

I took a deep breath, then took my binoculars out of my bag and focused through the night's darkness toward the hotel. From here, I could see straight into the room.

And right there, dead center of the window was a nice handsome face clearly visible just above the thin gold strap and tawny shoulder brushed by the wisps of magnificent blonde tresses that belonged to my gravy train. They were both on the couch, him facing me and her facing him. He was a good-looking guy with wide shoulders and a narrow waist, shaped like a "V" with muscled arms. He had a square jaw and dark blue eyes. He wasn't yet an A-lister, but quickly working his way, or rather fucking, his way up.

Kemper Lance, recent Grammy Award winner, had her back toward me, as I mentioned, but anyone could recognize the most famous backside in Hollywood. Her fancy gown, scooped all the way to her lower back, right above the crack of her ass, leaving very little to the imagination. Mr. Handsome Whatshisname didn't look like he had much imagination behind his attractive but bland facade. I wouldn't be surprised if she was completely bare beneath the dress. Going commando is really quite popular with the young, hottie set today, so long as the skirts are long enough to cover the sweet spot when they climb in and out of cars.

Kemper tossed her hair over her shoulder, leaned in, and touched his arm. She was probably about to fall out of her dress and even though her singing ability earned her awards and lots of money, she was not as famous for her body of work as she was for her body, particularly after that hot little sex tape was "leaked" to the Web by her best friend and costar, Ainsley Aoilin. The perfect bell shape with slim waist and dangerous curves said that this little pop starlet had grown up from the pigtailed kiddie she used to be to the talented temptress she was today. She knew it, too.

Her face kept pointing away from me as she moved forward, circling his neck with her hand, and as her head started to block my view of him, I saw him close his eyes. If she ate her favorite garlic and onion dressing on her salad with dinner, I hoped he could close his nostrils, too. Everyone knew she ate that dressing because just last week there was a great shot of her stuffing lettuce into her lovely mouth with the headline "Kemper Lance, bombshell with killer breath."

Not very catchy, I felt, but then, not my headline. Not my photo, either, which is what had me out here, on this damn ledge.

It had been a long day and night getting here. When that shot of Kemper hit the press, my editor spent my lunch break screaming at me, suggesting that I was already a relic and ready for Social Security. Me, not even thirty yet, and my life as a tabloid photographer was plummeting to an end.

I'll admit I might have mellowed a little over the last few years.

The days of me swimming shark-infested water or crashing through windows for a money shot were over. But I still had brains, a sharp eye, and a great zoom lens on my camera. And can I really help it if every Tom, Dick, and Betty has a camera built into their phone today, so just about anybody out there can catch a shot of somebody doing something they shouldn't. My editor's point was that I could help it, that I had to help it, and if I didn't help it, then I could find a different job, preferably in Guam.

I switched from my binoculars to my camera, so I'd be ready. No crappy little camera phone for me. I had a Nikon zoom that would show me the hair in Kemper's nostrils if necessary, but only if she would turn around and show me that face.

Soon their kisses went from tentative pecks to tonsil hockey, but I still only could see the back of her head. He moved his hand down her back toward her firm ass and squeezed. The gesture seemed crude, but she apparently liked it. She pulled the straps of her dress off her shoulders, pushing them down, and then she shook her upper body at him.

At first, I was cold on the ledge. But things were heating up!

It wasn't the first time that my target was Kemper Lance. Four years ago my naked photos of her inside an upscale swing club were credited with causing her second divorce. And two years ago my before-and-after pics proved she had breast enhancements.

Kemper knew me well. And so did her fleet of security guards. I tried to make it to her fourteenth-floor hotel suite via the elevator, but they turned me around before I could say "going down." It was the same scene with the stairs. I might have tried to scale the outside wall, but my superhero outfit was at the cleaners.

This apartment building, just across the street, was my only chance for the shot. But the roof was too high, and I could only see knees. Yet the ledge, floating out there in the brisk breeze, was nearly perfect. I had a full view of both the bed and the couch.

By the time I focused the camera, they were already naked and stretched out on the sofa. It seemed that he didn't waste time on foreplay. I mentally cheered for him to take her doggy style, so I could get her whole face scrunched up in orgasm. Wishful thinking. The prude started missionary, and I only got a few shots of Kemper's ankles wrapped around his back.

He fucked her hard and fast in a monotonous rhythm. After a few minutes, he stopped. Damn him. I didn't get a single decent shot.

I was relieved when they moved to the bed. He wasn't as quick and useless as I assumed. I tried to catch Kemper as she walked by the window. I did catch a good look at her round breasts and hard nipples. Fake but beautiful. I didn't get more than her profile, though.

He stretched on his back, his legs hanging off the side of the bed and his massive hard-on pointing at the ceiling. I guess Kemper was a size queen and now it was clear to me why he was rocketing to the top of Hollywood when his acting skills were less apparent. I took a few shots of it . . . I mean, him. Maybe one of the European tabloids would be interested.

She climbed on top of him, tossing her long hair over her shoulders. From this angle, I could only see her side: the smooth curve of her right hip, her strong thigh, a peek at her right breast, and little more.

She took all of him inside her, throwing her head back, and then began bouncing away perpendicular to his prone position. Her breasts were shaking and moved pretty nicely for silicone. She rode him hard and, just as I imagined, she was a tigress, fucking him hard enough to make the bed quake.

I shifted positions. My pants were definitely feeling uncomfortably tight. I took as many shots as possible, always searching for the right angle, always trying for that perfect straight-on shot of her face.

It might seem bizarre that I was getting hard, sitting out on this ledge, but the sex was hot, the woman is hot, and for some reason I can't seem to get any with a real woman, what with my weird hours and crazy job. Ever since the whole Princess Di thing, being in this biz just doesn't get me much play. I wasn't even out of high school at the time and I'm the one out on the ledge risking my life, not threatening anyone else's, but no one cares about facts like that.

She leaned back, balancing her weight on her ankles. I could see her flat stomach, but her wild hair covered most of her face. She took him deep, fucking him with long strokes, her body shaking with each thrust.

Jesus. If I kept watching her, I was going to explode, and my job was to keep watching. I unzipped my pants to get more comfortable. Kemper had amazing stamina, bouncing faster now, with her mane flying about in the air. It reminded me of her break-out video when she showed the world that she was no longer that sweet little girl next door, but had transformed into a belly-crawling, leather-wearing sex kitten. I balanced my camera with one hand. Probably a stupid decision, but I couldn't take it anymore. If I didn't get any release, I was going to have the worst case of blue balls ever.

Kemper leaned forward, propping her hands on his bare chest, and started to grind her hips around and into him. She was milking his big cock with her powerful muscles. I imagined her face twisting in concentration, in part because I still couldn't see it. It didn't take me long before with a few long stokes I was spurting come over the ledge. Feeling immeasurably better, I focused the camera again, and just in time to catch her throwing her head back with orgasm.

Her profile was pretty clearly outlined in the window and my camera started clicking, as I hoped she'd turn the rest of the way. It almost seemed like she was purposely teasing me. Finally, I got it. She stretched like a cat and climbed off his cock. Sitting on the edge of the bed, she picked up a cigarette and lit up. With that just-been-fucked look on her face, she looked right at me. My camera wailed, many times faster than a clock's second hand.

But, what was this? Kemper was sticking her tongue out at me. And, then, shit. It wasn't Kemper at all. It sure looked like her, with her build, color, and hair, but when I saw the breasts, I should have known. They had bounced like they were real because they were real. This wasn't Kemper. It was her stand-in, who worked her videos with her, doing her stunts and occasionally body-double work. The woman who would stand in for shots where all you see are Kemper's back or partial profile and Kemper doesn't feel like having to stand there herself because her time's too precious to actually bother with scenes that don't show her face or follow her lip-synching lips.

The double was hunched over and trembling, shaking. No, she was laughing. Laughing at me as she showed me her middle finger.

Suddenly, a row of flashing lights hit me from the roof above. Then giggles. A short stream of liquid, smelling like gin, poured onto my shoulder and down my back. I peeked up and saw a crowd of faces hanging over the roof's ledge. I recognized only one—Kemper Lance. The rest? It looked to me like her entire entourage.

They kept laughing it up as they shouted down insults and jokes at my expense. They had me. She was smarter than I thought, and it would appear a whole lot more pissed off at our history than I'd imagined. She must have gotten word that I was on the prowl for her. She had her bodyguards going in and out of the hotel, and in retrospect, they were a bit obvious about it. They were just setting the bait and I bit. She arranged the entire thing, figuring out exactly where I had to go to try for a money shot.

It was a setup. An ambush. And a damn good one, though I doubted my editor would see anything funny about it. And, really, the taunts and insults weren't my biggest problem. My biggest problem wasn't even trying to get a money shot of Kemper Lance or explaining to anyone why I was caught fucking getting off on a two-foot ledge.

Nope. My biggest problem was getting off that fucking two-foot ledge.

Justine Baum

Erotic is to tickle the girl with a feather, kinky is when you use the whole damn chicken.

The Ties That Bind

Tyler and I have been together for six years, six good, stable, pleasant, respectful, nice years.

He's exactly the man I decided I wanted. A talk-show guest doc once suggested making a list of what you want in a person because then you're much more likely to get those qualities. I made my list: kind, attractive, in good shape, funny, *stable*. The doc was right. Tyler is all of these, especially stable. No matter what's going on with me, no matter what kind of tirade I'm having, he's *stable*.

Obviously he's a keeper but, well, I'm a bit bored, especially, and unfortunately, in the bedroom.

Enter daytime TV once again.

Yesterday, a sex therapist specializing in spicing up *stable* relationships was the guest. Naturally, I honed in on what she had to say. She was talking about inventive ways to use household items in the bedroom. Who knew that a whisk could do that? Not me. What piqued my interest, though, was the discussion on fabric. The show gave a whole new meaning to shopping for me.

Taking the rest of the day, I headed downtown to shop. I was amazed to feel turned on just fingering the material on a blouse. My imagination was on overload. Each time I touched an item I could hear the clerk in my head saying, "I know what you are going to do with that, you naughty, dirty girl."

Late in the afternoon, I ended up at Ralph Lauren in the men's department. There I found them, yards and yards of beautiful, luxuriant, decadent *ties*. Looking at them, I could barely contain myself. I fondled and caressed and stroked these ties and then I bought and bought and bought some more.

At home, I laid the ties on the bed. There was literally a smorgasbord of material. I couldn't help myself. I stripped off my clothes and rolled around on the ties. Feeling the material on my bare skin made me hot, hot and wet.

It was 5:30. Tyler always comes home at 6:00, never more than five minutes off either way. That left thirty minutes to prepare.

Hopping into the shower, I lathered up. Running my hands along my body, I slipped first one and then another finger inside me. The inside of my vagina felt like silk, like the silk of the ties, soft, smooth, pliant. I almost came right then. I pinched each nipple, then fingered myself some more. "No time to play now," I admonished myself.

With fifteen minutes to go, I dried off and attached four ties to the old brass bed my mother gave to me. Wouldn't she have been surprised to know what I planned to do with it? I left a bright paisley and a blue silk rep out. I had special plans for them.

Ten minutes to six had me closing the drapes as I lit cinnamon candles around the room.

Five 'til the hour and I lotioned and powdered myself and then threw on Tyler's old robe.

6:01 and I heard the back door open. Good, stable Tyler was home and right on time. Walking into the kitchen, I acted as though nothing was up.

"How'd your day go, hon?" I asked, kissing him on the cheek.

"Good," he said, pulling me close to him and kissing me on the lips. "Same old, same old. What's up? Don't you feel okay?" he looked at me in his old robe.

"I feel different," I replied casually. "Come into the bedroom, I'd like to show you something."

"What?"

"A present. Kind of."

"Cool."

Leading him into the dark, candlelit bedroom, I threw him down on the bed before he could say anything.

"Wha . . . ?" he tried, but too late.

Undoing his tie quickly, I looped it about his head, and gagged him. Grabbing his wrists, I tied each to a bedpost. I ripped off his shirt, popping buttons every which way, and then his pants. Shocked though he was, he was enjoying himself. I could tell immediately. His cock pushed up through the band of his underwear. By the time I pulled them down, a drip of moisture beaded the tip. I ran my tongue about the head and then engulfed him in my mouth. I heard him moaning through the gag.

With his shorts already off, I tied his ankles next. He tried to squirm. Taking the treasured paisley, I wrapped it around his balls like a cock ring and then attached it to the blue rep tie, which then in turn I looped about his neck. If Tyler moved too much the tie on his balls tightened.

He was trapped and he knew it.

Sitting on his face, I pulled the gag away and demanded: "Eat me!"

He leapt willingly to the task. His tongue went way up inside me, then came out and circled my clit. He did this over and over.

Before I came, I pulled away, gagging him again. Sitting on his chest, I pulled the paisley tie back and forth between my puffy lips. As I rubbed, it pulled tight on his balls. He moaned. Pleasure or agony, I was beyond caring. He was rock hard, so I knew it was working.

I removed the tie from his balls. Then I removed his gag. He sighed. As he opened his mouth, though, I balled up the wet paisley and stuck it in. I replaced his gag as he watched, wide-eyed in shock.

Slamming my aching pussy down over his swollen cock head until he was completely inside me, I rode him. Up and down. Up and down. Thinking to myself "God, I wish I had a riding crop. I'll have to remember that!" I grabbed his balls and slapped them gently.

I came and it was explosive. He moaned but I wasn't done. Coming again, I rocked back and forth, pulling a tie against his cock and my outer lips.

Tyler bucked and maybe screamed but I couldn't tell with the gag. Arching his back, he threw me up. I came back down on his cock. He came and his ejaculate flooded out into his pubes. I mopped it up with the closest tie and licked the ends. He watched me intently. I rode on and on, coming yet again. Releasing the tie from my mouth, I kissed him hard through his gag. I then collapsed on his chest, exhausted.

His cock fell out on his leg. I could hear his heart pounding. Gradually, I dozed off.

Waking a few minutes later, I did a cat stretch. Hopping off the bed, I went to start the shower. Tyler made some noises.

"I'm sorry, honey," I said, "I can't hear you, you have a tie in your mouth."

He bucked up and down and shook his head. In a fit of compassion, I removed the gag, kissing him again, gently this time.

"What has gotten into you?" he asked.

"Talk shows."

"God bless them."

"Amen," I said.

"So," slitting his eyes at me, he asked, "what's tomorrow's show about?"

J. J. Layton

JennaTip #7: Tie Me Up

Want to try it out? Of course you do.

You can start with ties, belts, scarves, torn strips of his ex's quilt she loves to death and left behind by accident . . . moving on. You can tie your partner to the bed, a chair, the banister, or even to the car bumper, but try not to get arrested by doing this in a public parking lot and whatever you do, don't drive off forgetting he's back there. You can also start by just tying your partner's hands together, which might be an easier way to get going.

You can buy specialty cuffs made of leather, metal, rubber, silk, or other synthetic and natural materials, like a nice cotton rope. They can have locks on them or be fairly easy Velcro release. If you do use silk or metal, be careful as both can tighten unexpectedly, restricting circulation, which is why it might be best to start off with cuffs made specifically for this sort of sex play. Also, be sure you don't tie the knots too tightly but leave about two fingers' worth of space between the rope and the wrist or ankle.

As with everything else, be sure to talk openly about what you're doing or planning to do, arrange for a safety word, a lot of people use "red" as in stoplight. Understand that to be tied up does require trust, so if you are tying someone up, be trustworthy and don't abandon them. At least not for longer than it might take for you to go get some chocolate syrup, whipped cream, a feather duster, and a bowl of ice. If you aren't sure what you need them for, then maybe you aren't ready to tie anyone up. Keep reading stories and learn what can be done with a blade of grass. Now that's kinky.

What a beautifully complex micro-story that drips with description. From the just right title to the twisted end, it's a quickie in the best sense.

Made to Fit

Knowing how visual he is, I chose the outfit particularly for him. It was entirely new, chosen to the stitch. I remember the first pair of heels he presented to me, the four-inch stilettos with the black patent leather and chrome metal spike for a heel. Oh, how I protested. But he persisted and I learned, even though I wobbled at first. Even through the blisters and the aches and the cramps in my arch and in my calves, I persisted.

Well, these heels are five inches. It was so difficult to find them in just the right style and size. But, I went online and searched and found the perfect pair. The heels are five inches, the arch incredibly high, and the bindings allow them to be tightened to cut so beautifully into the calves. They buckled with silver catches and the heels, like before, were beautifully polished, mirrorlike chrome.

The stockings were silk, gentle and strong. They were smoke black with seams tracing from the tip of the toe up the back, along the curve of the calf behind the knee to the thigh where they ended in wide bands of lace. They had no elastic to hold them up but were held in place by the garters of the lace and silk corset in silver and black, the silver reminiscent of the chrome of the shoe heels. The corset was a simple waist cincher, meant to create an hourglass curve with stainless steel spines for boning, allowing no leeway or breach but crushing all resistance, creating the body in its own image.

The lace and silk thong was simple and solid black. It was

never intended to draw attention or distract but to envelop the area, the crotch, the murky meeting of the legs, the thighs and the sex in shadow.

Before the stockings were slowly placed over the toe and smoothly unrolled up over the calves and knees to the mid-thigh, before the thong could embrace and obscure hidden delights, before the corset pulled and tied and pulled some more, and the shoes lovingly fitted, my darling had to be waxed. Yes, the outfit was for him, picked perfectly and exactly for him, and made to fit.

Adina Giordano

It takes two to tango but three to swing.

The Sins of Mary-Beth and Sue-Ellen

Law enforcement's different, up here on Blackstone Mountain. My jail's in back of my office and I bunk above. I've only got the one cell as what I try to keep free for the Saturday-night drunks. I don't have no room for real prisoners, nor the budget to feed 'em. If the crime's serious, like when Jake busted up the saloon and half killed old Amos, that's fine. He's doing six years in the county facility. It's the small stuff, misdemeanors and the like, what make a problem. There's no point in me settin' fines 'cause the folk up here are dirt-poor. That's why I got my own system of fines in kind. When Ike got drunk and run his truck through Miss Louise's shed, I fined him the lumber and labor to rebuild it, plus a dozen sacks of his new crop of taters—ten to compensate her and two for me, administration fee.

My way saves time, trouble, and paperwork. I know Billy-Bob takes a deer or ten out of season, and he knows I know, so he pays a regular fine of a decent-sized buck, all dressed, spring and fall. I give a hind to whoever's having a bad year and the rest goes in my freezer. Likewise, I don't go tramping through the Baker boys' back lot, sniffing for the smell of mash cooking. First day of every month, a gallon jug of prime shine appears on my stoop overnight. That's them paying their dues.

It ain't always so easy, though. Take the time the Rev. Sloane comes round to see me, ranting about them there "unnatural lusts." It seems like he paid a surprise call on Mary-Beth Calhoun and Sue-Ellen Baxter, who live up-mountain a ways. The way it came about that them girls live together was like this: The Calhouns and the Baxters had been feudin' for nigh on four generations. Neither clan was that good with a gun, but one way or another, they'd killed off each other's menfolk 'til there was just Jeff Calhoun and Jed Baxter left. I was hopin' that'd be an end to it, seeing as they'd both got married recent-like, to real pretty, and young brides.

It happened that those two idiots ran into each other, ridin' through Echo Valley. Even them two weren't fool enough to let off firearms, not in a place where a sneeze'll bring down an avalanche, so they went at it with fists and still managed to make such a ruckus, it tumbled a big boulder, two hundred feet down, right on top of 'em.

It had to be a double funeral, on account of, as Morty told me, the boys was inseparable by then. Mary-Beth and Sue-Ellen met up at the funeral. I was all braced for a catfight, but somehow, they took an instant shine to each other. A month later, Sue-Ellen moved in with Mary-Beth and we all heaved a sigh of relief.

Anyhow, Rev. Sloane wanted to offer his counseling services to the two gals in their time of mourning. He went on up the mountain to their place and he knocked and knocked on the girls' door but couldn't get no answer, so he just went on in. It seem the reason them girls couldn't hear him was on account of Mary-Beth's thighs was muffling Sue-Ellen's ears, and vice-versa.

Now Rev. Sloane's pretty good when it comes to preaching 'bout hellfire and the worm what never sleeps but he couldn't make those girls see what terrible sinners they were, not no-how. He said that as they didn't unnerstand what they did was immoral and a mortal sin, I should go on up and jaw the law at them. Well, I can't find no statute on the books that's against nuzzling pussy, not even if the owner of said pussy is a-nuzzling of yourn at the same time. The Rev. was hot for me to take action, though, and I didn't want him naming me from his pulpit. That's not good for a sheriff's reputation, so I drove on up as far as the trail went, then clambered up the rest of the way to the girls' cabin.

I guess I made more noise pushing through the brush than the Rev. had, 'cause the girls was waiting on the stoop, all excited-like to see me, and looking as cute and cozy as a pair of turtle-doves, 'cept doves don't have boobies and the girls sure did. I knew it on account of all they was wearin' was skirts they'd made out of Mary-Beth's aunt's old gingham curtains.

I don't know what was more consterning to me—having Sue-Ellen's big round boobies squish against my shirt as she hugged me, or watching Mary-Beth's lovely titties bob up and down as she jumped around. All I knowed is that it was gettin' darn hard, and I am talkin' 'bout my cock when I say it was hard. It was also hard to be angry and yet I'd promised to give 'em a real good talkin'-to an' I keep my promises, 'specially to the preacher.

Still, all 'n all, it wasn't easy, keeping my cock from twitchin', what with four long slender legs and two pairs of lush boobs on display in front of me on their old battered couch. It didn't help none that they squirmed so much, tucking a foot up under a delectable ass, or crossin' and uncrossin' their legs, giving me quick flashes of their sweet young pussies.

"So what did we do that was so wrong, Sheriff Luke," Sue-Ellen asked me, slyly. "We always thought that folks was supposed to be lovin' to each other."

"What's so bad about kissin'?" Mary-Beth wanted to know.

"There's kissin', and then there's kissin'," I tried to explain.

"Is this a sin?" Mary-Beth turned to Sue-Ellen and brushed their lips together.

"No."

"Is this?" They hugged and kissed with their lips parted and far enough apart that I could see a pair of sinuous tongues slip and slide over each other.

I croaked, "Yes."

"And if I stroke Mary-Beth's cheek"—she caressed her friend's face—"that's okay, but if I—" Her hand dropped lower. Her palm cupped Sue-Ellen's gorgeous left breast. Her thumb flicked a pert little nipple.

"That's getting a mite naughty."

The two little teases exchanged looks, got up, and came across to where I was, to sit one of them astride each of my knees. Mary-Beth loosened my tie. Sue-Ellen planted a soft kiss on my cheek.

"But them things is okay to do with men, right?"

"Kissin' boys is fine, at your age. You're both widders, after all, and no-one's 'spectin' you to be virgins."

Mary-Beth gave me a grin. "What if I was kissin' a man, even, like this—" Her mouth covered mine. I parted my lips to protest but couldn't speak on account of the honey-sweet tongue that lanced into my mouth.

Sue-Ellen completed Mary-Beth's question. "And I was to join in, like this." She pressed her face close. Before I knew it, there were two young tongues playing inside my mouth, one slidin' over mine, one slippin' under it.

When I was allowed to breathe again, Sue-Ellen continued, "Then we'd be kissin' a man at the same time as we kissed each other. Would that make it okay?"

Mary-Beth continued, "And how about—" She took my right hand and put it on her friend's left breast.

Sue-Ellen guided my left hand to Mary-Beth's right breast. As I squeezed and caressed, automatic-like, they each put a hand on the other's free breast.

Part of me wanted to stop them, but only a little part. They slipped from my lap to kneel between my feet. Mary-Beth tugged my zipper down. Sue-Ellen's warm hand slipped into my fly and pulled my cock out.

"You tell us if'n we doin' somethin' bad, Lucas," Mary-Beth said as Sue-Ellen's hot young mouth closed over my drooling knob. The two wantons passed my cock backward and forward, taking turns suckin' and bobbin'. Mary-Beth favored slaverin' and gobblin' but Sue-Ellen preferred noddin' hard, buttin' the head of my cock agin the back of her throat.

I was getting real close to shootin' my load when the girls jumped up. Sue-Ellen knelt up on the couch, bum high, legs spread. Mary-Beth dragged me by my cock. She steered it to nudge the soft creases of Sue-Ellen's lovely little pussy. I had no choice, did I? I thrust. My full length slid in. I pounded, hard and fast. I guess Mary-Beth could read it on my face because just as I was about to come, she pushed her friend forward, off'n me. I think I started a strangled yelp of protest but she swooped down, lips parted, and finished me off in her enthusiastic mouth. I pumped and pumped until she was drooling cream from the corners of her lips.

Sue-Ellen asked me, "Is it a sin if I kiss my girlfriend like this?"

Mary-Ellen lifted her face, mouth wide open and full of my spew. Sue-Ellen bent over her. Mouth-to-mouth, they exchanged my cream back and forth, endin' by sucking the last few drops off each other's tongues.

I tucked in and zipped up. "You know you've sinned real bad, don't you."

"Gonna put handcuffs on us and drag us down to your cell?" Sue-Ellen asked and she sounded almost like she liked the idea.

I was tempted, but the thought of what these two might get

up to come Saturday night, in a cell full of drunks, stopped me from takin' them up on the suggestion.

"You'll have to be punished," I said. I took them both by the hair and dragged them to the chair, where I dumped them over my knees, north and south, bums in, heads out. My left hand came down on Sue-Ellen's curvaceous bottom. My right slapped Mary-Beth's smooth young globes. They giggled until I'd counted a dozen slaps each. By twenty they were wrigglin' and sobbin'. I kept spanking until my palms got sore, and my hands are pretty-well hard an' covered in calluses.

"Let that teach you a lesson," I said, as they wiped away their tears. "But it ain't gonna keep you from sinning, is it?"

"No," they both confessed.

"Then I'll be back, the first and fifteenth day of each month, to make you pay for your sinfulness."

"Yes, please!" they chorused.

Like I said, law enforcement is different, up here on Blackstone Mountain. It ain't a bad life for a sheriff, though. There's fresh venison twice a year; a jug of 'shine each month, and twice a month, there's Mary-Beth and Sue-Ellen for me to try to teach decent morals.

Kate Whitfield

JennaTip #8: Oh! Spank Me, Part 2

Is spanking about control or domination? Is it about pain? Is it about needing the emotional release of being punished for transgressions? The answer is "yes." And also, the answer is that it depends. It depends on how you come to it. Do you seek to dominate your partner, to punish them for their sins? Do you want to submit and feel humiliated?

For some people the dynamic is completely different. It can be about play and be good and pleasurable without being about discipline, punishment or anything other than the sensations. And for the same people it can be about discipline on another occasion where there is a power exchange and a feeling of a need for remorse, closure, letting go of hurt or anger.

Again, it just all depends on the people involved in spanking. Therefore, if you want to try it out the first thing you should do is talk about it with your partner or if you do not have a partner and are considering instead advertising for a spanking or visiting a spanking club or event, consider why you want to be spanked, what you really want out of it, and if it is a part of foreplay or maybe you just want to be spanked without it being erotic or sensual.

Just as with so much you might want to try and do in your life, understanding what you really want, understanding why you really want it, and understanding how you can get it are really the important questions to answer. Once you know, then you can find the right person because you'll know how to explain exactly what it is you are seeking. If you are in a relationship already, knowing what you want and why can help you introduce it to your partner with your reasons and explanations.

Isn't it so very true that what is forbidden us becomes our obsession? Until I determine to give up chocolate, I can take it or leave it, but once it is off the menu, I have cravings like a junkie for a fix. Six days without an orgasm isn't fun, but it hardly merits forty days and nights in a desert, yet the very fact of its denial causes it to loom large and overshadow all everyday acts and events. Writhe with our heroine as her countdown commences.

Debased

It was absolute hell! Randy had gone and left me alone for six and a half days. Actually it was six days, eight hours, and forty-seven minutes that he had been away. He'd had to go. It was business. It was torturous. And if it hadn't been arduous enough, before he left, he had left me with final instructions. I would say I promised, but that would be redundant. I didn't have to promise. His word is law. He's knows it and I know it. He told me, "No orgasms while I'm gone."

He, likely, had said it as an idle whim of no great significance. Yet, while to him, it is but a whim, to me it is the air I breathe. His whim is my life.

Perhaps, had he not said anything, I'd have masturbated a couple of times, to relieve tensions, to relax and enjoy. But because he'd forbidden me, each bath, every idle moment, and all my bedtimes became torture. The water of the shower didn't simply fall and cleanse me, it rained hot kisses on my aching nipples and teased my clit until my stomach was tied into knots. The feel of my shirt brushing my breasts, scraping my hard nipples left me close to tears. Again and again, my fingers would find themselves draw up under my top to my areola or snaking down into my panties to pull at my clit. Then I would freeze. Randy had not forbidden playing or touching, but he had expressly forbidden release. I was to suffer. I was to feel my lust for him, to wish to die and be reborn as only he can make me, and to endure for days, for hours, for minutes and seconds. Each tick of time lasting longer and being more painful to me until I curled up in my bed, shaking and sobbing for Randy to return. The aches had grown over that time. My nipples, desperate for his fingers, peaked and hardened and throbbed. My cunt was a hungry void that convulsed and dripped every time I thought of him, and that was a hundred times an hour. My ass became permanently clenched and refused to relax, demanding that I somehow make him appear and dilate it with his insistent fingers or rigid cock.

I'd slept in the last shirt he'd worn and I perfumed my bed with his cologne, though both rubbed salt into my raw need. The blue traces on my white bottom faded away, deserting me, leaving me without the souvenirs of him that consoled me.

Then he'd returned, not even an hour ago. I had been quivering with readiness. I'd risen early so as to have five full hours in which to primp and pamper myself. My mound was freshly pumiced. My nails, lips and nipples were wet-bright with a new shade of scarlet. My hair was burnished and perfumed and my face was painted to make me a wanton.

I'd chosen to wear white, to appear for him as a depraved virgin. The dress was thin cotton, with tiny cap sleeves and a neckline that scooped beneath my breasts and presented them as one of the gifts I was eager to give him. It was gathered at my waist and mid-thigh length, with a slit on each side to mid-hip. White stockings, tightly tied with matching ribbons and heeled sandals in a crimson that matched my lips. All in place to perfection and I'd been ready.

I'd knelt, trembling, my collar on my extended palms, for a full half hour before he'd returned.

His fingers beneath my chin lifted me, uncollared. "You look lovely. I'll collar you later, pet. I have urgent work to take care of. Until then, you are at liberty."

At liberty! "Liberty" was the last thing I wanted. Was he being cruel, leaving me suspended in a state of "not completely owned," or was he being kind, knowing that his buckling my collar would inflame my need into a consuming firestorm of lust?

Whichever, something in me twisted and writhed. If it hadn't been for his "I'll collar you later," sustaining me, I'd have lost my mind in a maelstrom of insane desperation.

Randy dropped his bags, marched to his semicircular desk, booted his PC and slipped a CD into the drive.

Didn't he know what I was suffering?

Of course he did. He knew everything. It was just his work. Randy was in "work mode." That always came first. Everything else, even me, was set aside, encapsulated, not allowed to exist until the work was done.

What could I do to placate the screaming vacuum in me? I was always to look appealing, whatever the circumstances. That was permitted and what Randy permitted was mandatory. Randy could split his mind. Most of it could be untangling a knotted plot and yet at the same time, another part could take pleasure in the way I posed at the edge of his line of vision. He'd told me that he might be rapt in his craft but the sight of me, beyond his screen, displaying myself seductively, still aroused part of him. The moment he "switched off," PC and "work mode," that lusting part expanded to become his entire being and then he focused on me with as much or more intensity as he had his work.

Very well! I wasn't allowed to distract the working part of him, but I could certainly prime the other, libidinous part.

At liberty? Fine. Then I was free to stand behind him and look over his shoulder. I was free to stand close enough that the back of his neck would feel the heat radiating from my cleavage.

He said, "Hmmm!" and leaned back to read what he had just written. As if not aware of what he did, he snuggled his neck between my breasts, paused, and leaned forward to type again.

He'd touched me! He'd done that before, when working. There were times when he'd studied a book with me at hand, kneeling beside him, and idly fondled my nipple without taking his eyes from the pages. Two minds, one intent on work, one aware of my skin's textures.

If I didn't ask for his eyes or his hands, he could type with some part of him in contact with my skin. I wouldn't have his focus but at least I could give him mine.

I circled his desk and crawled beneath it. My nervous and worshiping hands lifted his left foot and eased his loafer from it. He didn't stop me, so . . . I took his other shoe and set it aside. Delicately and deftly, I rolled one, then both socks from his feet. Now I had access to at least a part of him. I rolled onto my back and lifted his right foot. My head tilted back, angled the way he sometimes held it to fuck my mouth. My hands guided his foot, slowly, and inserted his big toe into my avid mouth.

The keys clicked, uninterrupted. I sucked. I made saliva and laved his toe. My tongue extended and wriggled between his big toe and his funny short second toe. Mmmm! The joy was two-fold, the taste of him and the self-inflicted subservience of my adoration. I reveled in the knowledge that whether my collar was on or not, only a slut-slave of the deepest degradation could take intense pleasure from such humble service to her owner. Warmth infused me. I was depraved for him and proud of it.

I suspended his foot above my face and showered kisses and

licks from toe to heel and back again. I was under his foot, beneath him, as I should be. It was the lowliest position to which I could aspire. My lips engulfed his toe again, sucking and licking and mumbling on it, wetting it, wetting it more. I wanted it to drip with my saliva.

Bold with lust, I writhed on my back, inching closer to him, until I was looking up at the underside of his seat. If only it had been transparent, and him naked! Looking up at his ass and his balls would have . . .

I shuddered with need.

I steered his foot to my breast, his toes to my nipple. By moving it from side to side, I flickered that wet toe over the peak. He had to feel that! Part of him had to, anyway. Was I succeeding in inflaming the nonworking part of his mind?

Now that one nipple was in contact with him, my cunt and clit screamed at me. I edged from under his chair, spun around on my bottom, and reversed my position. Knees bent and spread, feet as flat on the floor as my heels allowed, I took his foot in both hands, lifted my pussy to it and . . .

Oh yes! His wet toe was on my straining clit, then down and another wriggle and the toe was nudging my swollen lips, and between them, and it was inside me!

I wasn't permitted a climax until he said so, but I could still fuck his foot! Oh! Oh! I dragged and squirmed, weaving my lifted hips from side to side as I worked one toe, two, four, five, in, then deeper, grinding and spreading my engorged flesh until I had half of his foot in the soft tight warm wet pocket of my sex. The knuckle of his big toe came exactly to my G-spot so that if I twitched . . . Fuck! That sensitive spot warmed and glowed, sending messages of "lubricate" deep up inside and I needed! Oh how I needed to . . .

The clicking stopped. Two more clicks, "screen off," "speakers off." His foot pulled back, tugging out of me with an obscene squelch.

"Clean your juices off my foot," he said.

I turned again, mouth to toe, and sucked my own essence off his toes.

"You've made me very hard, Lace."

I said, "Thank you, Randy." I reached up and laid a gentle hand over the hot rigidity that tented his pants. "May I . . . ?"

"No. After a week without you and what you have just been doing, I'd come too soon. This is going to be long and hard, Lace. I am going to give you a great deal of pain before I use you for my release. You are going to earn my climax ten times over before I grant it to you."

"Thank you, Randy."

"I am going to make myself suffer, Lace. You, and the things I will do to you are going to make my need unbearable before I give into it. I'm going to shower, now. Take the long black leather case I brought back up to the bedroom. Wait there for me, with your collar. It is going to be a very strenuous night, my precious pet."

I almost skipped up the stairs. One thought was chiming in my head. His self-control was absolute but nevertheless, his lust for me made him suffer, just as mine for him made me.

Tracy Randolph

JennaTip #9: Orgasm Denial / Orgasm Control

Orgasm denial is a wonderful way to exert power and control in a dominant/submissive relationship. It is generally considered safe without any real negative effects. However, continued denial may have some negative impact for men since it denies them the positive health benefits of orgasm. For example, it has been suggested that frequent orgasm does reduce the likelihood of prostate cancer. To counter this issue a man's prostate can be "milked" without his experiencing the release of orgasm, draining him of his ejaculate. This is a complex procedure and more detailed than can be provided in a quick tip.

Orgasm control is like orgasm denial except that the intention is to encourage tension build up prior to release for increasingly powerful orgasms. The only real negative is fewer orgasms, but the payoff is in bigger and more powerful release. Also, there is something to be said for the anticipation of a coming "coming," so to speak.

Being put on a no-orgasm notice for a week or until a next meeting or for any time frame, perhaps just for the next three hours, heightens the desire and can raise the sexual excitement to an obsessive level. As mentioned, waiting does not have to be for days, the build-up time frame can be just hours or being brought to the brink and then made to wait, to hold off on release.

Play around with orgasm denial and control with your willing partner. It's a great way to play at domination and to exert power with such positive results.

Who wouldn't love to get all painted in green and brown,
jump into the briars, and roll around in the muck for
a nice hard fuck?

Love and War

I was more used to black mascara and blue eye shadow than the black and blue marks I had all along my shins from smacking my legs against low-lying limbs. With the brown and olive drab grease that masked my face and my tinsel blonde hair shoved mercilessly up under the brown ball cap, I was unrecognizable. Hopefully, I was invisible as well or I'd be dead.

The clothes, well, the clothes were awful, army surplus, a patchwork of brown and green blotches and rough against my tender skin.

I'd been patient for over an hour, though it seemed more like days, crouched in a bed of green leaves and brown thorns, to match my outfit. The mesh of bush and vine stretched out, taking up as much area as a parking space and as high as the brim of my cap. I was on a small mound, overlooking a thin trail that wound through the woods like a garden hose. It was painful moving around. Each twist inevitably led to several spiked barbs jabbing into me. Who else would be stupid enough to hide in here?

I didn't have anything to do but occasionally inspect my pistol. I'd checked it a dozen times. And each time, it was clean, loaded and ready to trigger.

Finally, I saw him. He was wearing the same camo clothes as I, but with a brown leather cowboy hat atop his head, a handsome man, thick arms, wide shoulders, and a waist so thin that he could have been a stripper. He was being cautious. He'd jog the trail for a few steps, then dive behind the safety of a tree, swiveling his neck around like an owl, holding his own pistol at the ready. There was too much at stake here for either of us to relax. But in my experience, men are generally lazy creatures, and after a few minutes of this dash-and-duck maneuvering, this one proved it by using the trail, rather than the safety of the shielding forest. Just as I'd hoped and planned.

He was near enough for me to spit on, hugging a pine and looking away toward the sound of a bird when I crashed upward through the briars, aimed, and fired twice. The first shot hit his heel. The second hit the tree. I fired again as he turned and hit him square in the chest. The capsule exploded, covering his shirt with red paint.

"Goddamn it, Christy." He pulled off his goggles and slapped them against his thigh. "How long you been hiding there?"

"Sucka. I win."

Jim and I'd been together for over three years. To keep things spicy, we'd started trying new adventures like sailing, extreme traveling, gambling, and paintballing. He'd won the first two times we went, but not this time.

"How did you even get in there?" He was searching to find some way that I'd cheated.

"Shut up. You're dead." Actually, I wasn't even sure how I'd gotten into the prickly patch. Worse. I had absolutely no idea how I was going to get out.

I thought maybe I could jump out in one quick, painful motion and it would be over. I tried, but the vines grabbed my feet and I landed facedown. I struggled as the briars bit into me. The shoulder of my shirt, and the thigh of my pants, ripped loudly as I tried to snake to the edge.

"Shit, Jim. Help me."

He was nonchalant when he spoke, "Sorry, Christy. I'm dead. Remember?"

Eventually, I escaped. That was when Jim, finally, came over and offered me his hand.

"Nice job. Time for lunch?"

"Lunch? What the hell do you mean, lunch?" I slapped his hand away. "It's time for my reward."

"Here?" He looked around, acting like the owl again. "Now?"

"It didn't stop us the times when you won. Now strip down and lay your ass back on the ground." I won, damn it. And that meant I got to be on top. He'd have to suffer with the dried leaves and bugs biting at his back.

"But there are other people out here. Playing their own games." I let him talk all he wanted, while I unbuckled his belt. I pulled the strap free from its loops, and tossed it into the briar patch.

"Oh, shit, Christy. Who's going to get that?" he whined. I went for his zipper next, tugged it down, and my hand brushed against his cock. Well, well—while his voice was saying no a very important part of him seemed to say an aggressive yes.

We kissed wildly, as our camouflage paint mixed. His pants fell down as I worked on his shirt buttons. Free, I snapped the shirt behind him until it snagged on his elbows.

"Christy . . ." his whine had turned into a moan. And that's when seven Judo classes came into good use. I stuck a leg behind his knee, pushing his shoulders until he fell back onto the bare earth.

My clothes came off fast. And then I met him, my thighs to either side of his hips, my palms smudging his nipples.

"Oh, shit."

There were a dozen of them. Other gamers, walking down the trail toward us. They must have just finished their game, as they laughed and spoke and tramped along, not caring who saw or heard them.

"Oh, shit," Jim repeated as he struggled to get out from beneath me. This was going to be embarrassing. There was no way we could dress in time.

I was first. I grabbed all my clothes, my pistol, and whatever else I could, then leapt knees-first back into the briar patch. Jim only had time to pull on his pants, before he followed me in. His body crashed into the thorns and a mild yelp burst through his lips as he came to a halt beside me.

The others heard the yelp and stopped. A few of them scanned around, but the briar patch, settled, kept us concealed.

"Hey, I found my belt," Jim whispered.

"Hush," I commanded in a louder whisper.

A few minutes later the group had moved beyond us and out of sight.

So, there we were, in varying stages of undress and trapped in that little briar patch. Our skin looked like road maps of thin, red lines. We couldn't dress without the thicket pushing us back into each other's arms. But we could laugh. And we did. And we could kiss. And we did that, too. We'd be there until we worked up enough courage to bolt out. Until then, we didn't have much safe space, but we had enough for me to take my reward.

Ramo Kye

I've had my share of fun in the back of limousines—heck, in the back of Toyotas, too—but nothing to match this story. And here I thought I had experience.

Stretch Limo

I pressed my palm against my mound, securing the flapping silk of my wrap as best I could. My other hand clutched it between my breasts. A soft summer breeze ruffled the wrap behind me, flirting with my bottom, perhaps exposing it? The click of heels behind me paused for a moment before continuing. Had I given some woman a cheap thrill?

When was I going to be picked up? My eyes strained against the blackness of my blindfold. The sun, that had to be setting by now, warmed the exposed skin of my neck and the gentle slopes of my barely covered breasts.

A car purred and stopped. Although blind, I could sense something bulky in front of me as a hand, suede-gloved, touched my elbow.

The voice that accompanied the touch whispered across my cheek like a lost tune in the wind. "The door is open, Miss. Just step up and in. I won't let you fall."

I extended my long leg tenuously, touched my toe on something that gave a little, fumbled, and found firmness at the level a car's floor might be. I abandoned all attempts to hold my wrap in place, felt for the edges of the door, and somehow clambered into the soft leather interior. The car moved away almost immediately.

Delicate fingers took my hand. Erin's husky voice said, "Move over to your left a bit, would you. There's a dear."

Hands steered me gently but decisively. I felt three hands on me and realized that Edgar was in the car, too. They moved me to face the back of the car. Clearly, this was a stretch limo and not simply a town car as I'd presumed. I slid down the buttery leather until my bottom met a narrow shelf that was seat-high but somewhat uncomfortable for sitting. It was not something organic to the car, but an after-market addition that had to have been made especially for Edgar and his purposes.

Erin said, "I'll fasten your belt for you, Lizette."

What clicked decisively felt more like a metal band, a circle like a bangle bracelet.

"It's too tight!" I breathlessly dared to complain.

"Nonsense," Edgar said. "It's been adjusted to your measurements. I made certain that it'd be exactly two inches tighter than snug."

"Tighter than snug? I didn't know snug was so exact," I dared impudently.

"We'll be fitting you with corsets later. It's time you got used to a little constriction." And with that he slapped my face, quite hard, for my impertinence.

Corsets? The thought of being bound took my breath away more than the band around my waist . . . or the slap.

A hand took my right wrist and held it out sideways. Another metal band clicked. Then it was the turn of my left wrist. The hand that took my right ankle had to be Edgar's again. It lifted out to the side and pulled. I felt myself being dragged around with it until only the right cheek of my bottom was half on the shelf-seat. I'd have fallen if it hadn't been for the solid restraints. Even so, my leg wasn't meant to go the way he was forcing it. Damn, it was held as high as my bottom and straight out to the side. I could feel the strain in my groin.

Oh no! Now he had my left ankle and was . . . No . . . No! I had to say it aloud. "No. Please? You can't spread me like this."

But he could. His grip and the pressure were inexorable. My tendons were tugged until I thought they would snap. The spreading was parting my sex, opening it into an oval. Just as it seemed the pain was unbearable—click!

"There," Edgar said with satisfaction.

"She looks like a frog pinned out on a card," Erin observed.

"A pretty little girl-frog, all ready for us to dissect."

"The wrap spoils the picture," Erin complained.

Edgar said, "Then take care of it, Erin."

"Thank you, Edgar."

Cold steel touched my shoulder. I shivered. Snip. Scissors. Oh, if Erin cut my wrap away, the only clothing I had, I'd be left with nothing. What if they put me out on the street, naked?

Snip, snip, snip. Silk parted. My sleeves hung in pieces. The flap over my breast fell away. Someone tugged. The silk slithered from me. I was totally bare.

Cold metal bracketed my right nipple! The blades of the scissors! Oh no!

Edgar growled, "No, Erin!"

Bless him!

"I wouldn't really," Erin whispered. "You know that, Edgar. I wouldn't spoil her. I was teasing. See how it stiffened that cute nipple?"

The next sound from Erin's lips was a pained grunt. "I'm sorry, Edgar! I didn't mean anything. Don't do that again, please?"

"You want to change places with Lizette?"

"And have to endure the same things that you have planned for her?"

He chuckled. "I know you'd volunteer for that, Erin. No. If you change places you'll just sit there, restrained, while I play with our new toy. You wouldn't be touched. All you'd have to amuse you would be the sounds that Lizette would make while I enjoyed her."

There was a pout in Erin's voice as she said, "I'll be good, Edgar."

"I know you will. You're not a fool. Now, don't be selfish. Pour the girl some champagne."

There was a "pop" and the sounds of pouring. Glass touched my lip. I drank gratefully.

Something touched the hollow inside my left thigh. It was too gentle to be sure but I hoped it was Edgar's finger. I gurgled to show my pleasure. Something frigid and wet was pushed against my left nipple. I jerked. Wine spilled from my lips.

"That was clumsy," Edgar said in a warning voice. "Erin, clean her up and spank her."

"Thank you, Edgar."

I tensed and then relaxed. Even though my bottom was tilted forward off that shelf, there was no room for anyone to spank it.

The warmth of a naked body came close, from my right. A nipple poked into the side of my breast. A hot tongue lapped across my lower lip. The mouth moved to my ear. Teeth nipped my lobe.

"Ready?"

"Ouch!" The fingers slapped against my pussy, again, and again. No, my ass couldn't be spanked, but my lips could, and being so open, each sharp sting landed on my wet inner lips. Erin clearly was an expert at this. Though each slap stung, it was just short of real pain and . . .

. . . and the heat and the tingling were spreading into my clit and it was soooo . . .

"Stop before she comes," Edgar ordered.

She stopped, leaving me teetering on the edge of an orgasm. I dared not speak but I moaned a plea.

My hair had tumbled over my face. Fingers brushed it back behind my ear.

"Look how big I've made her clit," Erin boasted.

It certainly felt big. It felt more exposed than it ever had before. If either of them were to touch it, perhaps I could get to where I needed to go.

Ice touched my naked sensitive nub, freezing it in that "almost coming" mode.

"Suck it just a bit bigger and then use this," Edgar ordered.

Hot lips melted the frigidity and pulled my poor aching clit out so very, very long. It was tugging at me, deep down inside. There was no way it could be drawn out any further.

Then I felt a sharp nip, just where the root of my clit went under my pubic mound. It felt like some sort of clip, gripping me there and it held my sheath retracted and my clit's shaft extended. My clit wouldn't be able to retreat, no matter what!

It wasn't just my clit that was exposed and defenseless. I was spread wide, restrained, mouth, nipples, anus as well as clit, exposed. They could caress, lick, suck, nip, bite, whatever they fancied, anywhere. There was nothing I could do to stop the most depraved indignities being performed on my body. I'd been transformed into a love doll. For this depraved pair, I was nothing but a sex toy, to be fondled or abused, then perhaps abandoned in a closet until their whim brought me out to be played with once more.

That thought, the thought alone, clenched my pussy, deep inside. A trickle ran from my sex.

"I need to come," Erin complained.

"Then take one climax, just one."

"One will leave me wanting more, Edgar. Please?"

"One or none."

"Oh, very well."

I felt moist body heat inches from my mouth. I inhaled woman-scent. My tongue stretched out.

"No tongue!" Erin said.

Puzzled, I pulled my tongue back. Something smooth touched between my lips. Fingers clamped behind my head, tangling in my hair. It was Erin's clit. It was so long and rigid like a miniature cock. She squished the head of it between my lips, then she took one hand from my head and pressed my lips closed, pinching them around her clit. Then she started pushing against me and pulling away, quickly. Oh fuck! Erin's clit was fucking my lips! I'd never felt so damned used. The way she held my head and my lips, and the way they had me spread before them, unable to move had I wanted to, I had no choice. It degraded me and thrilled me.

The thrusting accelerated. Erin was grunting. Faster! She shoved hard, splaying her cunt's lips over my mouth. She ground, rotating, washing my face with a flood of juice.

When the pressure eased, I licked my lips but a warm mouth splayed over mine, sucking hard. Erin was taking her come back, licking it off my face.

Edgar said, "Take one stocking off, Erin."

The sounds painted a picture in my mind. A "ploomph" as Erin dropped back into the bench seat followed by a clicking sort of noise as she kicked a shoe off and then a subtle rustle as she rolled a stocking down and off.

Then the Erin-smell again and something fluttered across my face. The gossamer touch drifted to the hollow of my throat. It teased across my left nipple. Almost too softly to be felt, it slithered over my tummy and came to rest draped over my straining outstretched thigh.

"There will be more of that, later," Erin promised.

There was a flurry of bewildering touches. Ice on my nipple, navel, clit. Hot, almost hurting hot, oil, dripped on my other nipple, my clit, in the hollow of my throat. Strokes and pinches, sucking kisses, nips and nibbles, here, there, and everywhere. Erin's voice husked obscenities into my right ear. Edgar murmured depravity into my left.

A tongue touched my mouth, at its left corner. Another touched the right. Both worked in to meet mine. One slid over, the other under. As I returned the double-kiss, it was whisked away. Edgar's fingers squeezed my jaw apart. Spit dribbled into my open mouth. I shuddered, adjusted, and before I could swallow, both tongues returned, lapping it out.

And they pinched my nipples. A gentle oiled finger rotated on my clit. And they pinched the delicate hollows of my thighs. And they licked behind my ears, and teased my nipples, and hurt them a little, and kissed them better, and . . .

The sensations came at me so quickly, from everywhere, invading everywhere until my head was spinning, as though I'd had a magnum of champagne and not just a sip. Their expert teasing kept me on the very edge, desperate for release. Lust ripped through me, built to a fist inside my belly, in my womb. My clit and nipples strained. My anus clenched. A madwoman, inside my head, babbled desperate need.

Everything suddenly stopped. I sucked air.

"A blade of grass?" Edgar suggested.

The tiniest tickle probed into my rectum, making me crave for something stiff and thick.

"A petal from the rose?"

Smooth softness wrapped the naked head of my exposed clit and was manipulated on it. Erin said, "Your cock is stiff and leaking, Edgar. I really must taste you. I need to, please, Edgar. May I?"

"You shall," he promised, "but not directly. I'm going to open the roof."

There was a click and a sliding sound. Air, smooth and warm as baby's milk, fluttered my hair. I felt body heat and smelled man-smell. Something hard, hot and wet touched my cheek. Before I could twist my head to suck on it, it was gone.

"Give it to *her*, Erin," he said. "Open wide, with your tongue extended, Lizette."

I obeyed. The head of his cock, dripping pre-come, touched my tongue. Much as I yearned to curl the few drops back into my mouth, I held still. The subtle soft slithery noises of Erin masturbating Edgar's cock tantalized me.

His cock's head beat on the tip of my tongue, flipping it fast, then faster.

"Come for us, Edgar!" Erin demanded. "Come, please? Come for us? We want it, don't we, Lizette?"

I made assenting noises, keeping my tongue stretched.

Edgar grunted, deep and guttural. Erin moaned a plea that turned into, "Yes! It's coming. Ready, Lizette?"

I nodded. Rich warm foam flooded my tongue. His cock's head slid through it, pushing it into my mouth. I clamped my lips on its shaft and sucked, and sucked, and sucked.

Erin ordered, "Don't you dare swallow!"

I held it, thick and delicious, in my mouth. The cock retreated. Wet lips spread over mine. A tongue probed. I let it in. My tongue, and Erin's, dabbled in Edgar's spending, savoring. Little by little the heady liquid disappeared.

The limo decelerated. Edgar announced, "We're here."

I had no idea where here was. I had no clothes and I was manacled in a limo. I was blindfolded. My heart was racing.

"Welcome to our country home, Lizette. Now we can begin your training in earnest."

In earnest? Did that mean that what I'd endured so far was just hors d'oeuvres? What on earth would be required of me when they got to the main course?

Fingers released my wrists, arms, ankles, and waist. The sudden freedom, the rush of blood back into cramped muscles, proved too much. I collapsed in a heap at Edgar's feet—where I realized, at long last, I belonged.

Tracy Randolph

JennaTip #10: Supersized Clit

Clitoris sizes vary from woman to woman just as penis size varies or eye shape and color or skin tone or hair color and texture all vary from person to person. The private parts are just as unique as any other parts and should be embraced (literally sometimes) for being special. If everyone looked the same or tasted the same, it wouldn't be as interesting a world. A clit might be long or larger than average for different reasons, possibly due to hormone exposure in the womb, but notice that instead of using a word like "normal" the word used is "average." Average just means that some are smaller and some are larger but by and large most fall within a certain range.

Do yourself a really big favor when looking at your body. Don't get caught up in "normal" and "abnormal" about your private parts any more than about any part of your body or even your imagination. In the end, having a functioning working healthy body means you have a normal body no matter the shape, size, or color. And if you happen to fantasize about women with long clits who can ejaculate, as she did in the story then keep in mind that that's normal, too.

Fantasy and imagination are gifts to excite and stimulate us. You might have fantasies you would never enjoy as reality. That's why they are fantasies. It's doubtful many people would really like a tentacle-waving squid thing from outer space as a sexual partner in reality but thousands do in their fantasies. Just check out some of that erotic romance alien literature that abounds or watch some old Star Trek shows.

This is a little bit about large clits in that, yes, they do exist, but this is more about how normal a big clit or a dark pink pussy or brown nipples or green eyes are and how healthy it is to accept the beauty in diversity and embrace what is unique and amazing about each person than wish to be homogenized into an all-bland society of dittoheads, strip malls, and minivans, no offense to the soccer moms getting their freak on with these awesome JennaTales.

Don't just be you, be a happy, sexy, unique you.

Beware! This story has one of the most erotic bondage scenarios that may have you running to the medical supply store for lots and lots of gauze. Do you already have a metal straight-back chair?

Gift Wrapped

Ten years of marriage, ten years of comfort, ten years of psychological security, what do they all add up to? Well, in my estimation, ten years of lessening libido. Welcome to the state of marriage in the twenty-first century, or at least to the state of *my* marriage. Gone are the lust-blurred nights and early morning romps. Gone, too, weekends when we lived under the covers of our double bed, surfacing only for food or drink. Now we have a king-size bed, but good-natured affection has replaced naked lust. Instead of heat, we have something called warmth.

I still have memories of the animal scent that sticks to your body and clings to your hair even after you shower, but those memories are dimming, and I fear someday they will disappear altogether.

The last time I had sex with Gary was on my birthday, and that was over three months ago. Gary is definitely still attractive to me. But he hasn't had time to breathe since he got on the partner track at the firm. He's not unaware of our dismal sex life. Only last night he finally addressed the issue himself. He said for his birthday, tomorrow, he wanted me to surprise him. It could be whatever I wanted, but he wanted the gift to reawaken our sex drive, somehow. *Whatever I wanted.* Those three words have been echoing in my head all day.

Tonight Gary is going to get the birthday surprise of his life. Tonight I'm going for broke. Today I was teaching school, but tonight's lesson is adult rated. I'm going to recreate a scene for Gary that I saw in a Japanese bondage magazine when I was eighteen, a scene that has been the source of my favorite fantasy for many years. Only one person in my life knows about this secret fantasy and that's my best friend, Melissa. I've known Melissa for years. We grew up together, and now we teach at the same elementary school, and the reason Melissa knows about this fantasy is because she was the one who showed me the magazine in the first place.

To accomplish my fantasy tonight, I need her help. When I told Melissa on the phone what I wanted her to do, she laughed at first but then she said she wouldn't miss it for the world.

Now it's time. I'm sitting here stripped naked on a stiff-backed chair in the living room. Enter Melissa.

"Gary is going to be so shocked after I get you ready," she says.

"That's the goal," I reply. "At least one goal. Nothing less than a sexual earthquake is going to save my sex life."

Melissa is staring at my breasts, which are fairly full. OK. They're big.

"Hope I've got enough gauze to cover those puppies."

In keeping with the picture I saw in the Japanese bondage magazine, I've asked Melissa to wrap my body, leaving certain strategic areas exposed.

Slowly, Melissa begins. Starting with my feet, she winds the white gauze up each leg, stopping at the top of my thighs so it appears I'm wearing white thigh-high stockings.

Then, leaving my sex exposed, Melissa continues wrapping the gauze, starting above my pubic bone and spiraling around my abdomen and up my waist until she reaches the area beneath my breasts. Playfully she pinches my pink nipples, and I scold her. I'm straight and Melissa knows it. She's more "whatever." In order to coax her into helping me, she blackmailed me, the merciless wench, making me agree that as long as Gary did not object, she could watch . . . not participate . . . watch.

I'm getting a little nervous about that promise. Nervous because I don't know at all how Gary will react to any of this and nervous because I haven't been dripping wet from anticipation since I don't even remember, but it was a long, long time ago.

Continuing the wrapping, she binds the area above my breasts, leaving the nipples exposed. Then slowly she wraps each of my arms.

My mouth and throat she leaves bare. But my brown eyes she covers with gauze three times, wrapping the thick material tight around my short black hair. The world plunges into darkness, leaving me only my sense of touch, smell, and hearing. But Melissa's work is not yet over. Firmly she binds my arms and legs to the chair. Now I am powerless to move.

While we wait for Gary, Melissa describes the scene to me. I'm definitely aroused. A moment later I hear the front door open, and then I hear Gary's recognizable tread on the parquet floor of the hallway.

He calls out my name.

"I'm waiting in the living room," I call out.

Closer and closer Gary strides down the hallway, and then I hear a hoarse whisper of surprise as he enters the living room.

"My God!"

"I wrapped her all myself," Melissa announces proudly. "What do ya' think?" Gary is speechless, but I hear his footsteps coming closer.

"So, can I watch?" Melissa asks.

"Huh? Yeah. Whatever." Gary mumbles.

The very next moment Gary's mouth fastens on my left nipple, sucking it and biting it. I squirm, partly from the unexpected sensation, partly from the fact that I know Melissa is still in the room watching.

It isn't but a second, so quick I am barely registering the feel of his mouth on my breast, when he transfers silently to the other. My bereft left breast is chilled as the cool air prickles my skin. Gary's mouth has transferred to the other nipple, and his hand is searching for the warmth between my legs.

The decision not to bind my mouth or throat was to provide Gary access, but now I realize how desperately I need to open my mouth wide as I suck in gulps of air, moaning as I feel Gary's hand massaging my wet aching lips.

In a whisper, I ask Gary if he is pleased with his birthday gift, and he kisses me full on the mouth.

"That's your answer, baby."

He continues kissing me in a long languid kiss, his lips soft against mine, his tongue slipping gently into my mouth. I suck on his tongue.

"Just a suggestion of what this mouth can do," I say, breaking away.

His fingers drop down to explore me further, and my breathing comes short and sharp. From a corner of the room I hear a soft moan from Melissa. I know she's touching herself as she watches. I can imagine her hand under her skirt touching and teasing herself. Melissa gets louder as Gary slips his fingers into my mouth.

Next I hear Gary's zipper. My mouth waters at the sound.

Gary whispers for me to open my mouth, and I open it wide for him. He slides his fabulous cock inside my mouth. I suck happily. He starts moving in and out of my mouth. At the same time, his hand drops down between my legs again. His index finger begins playing with my clit. From the corner I hear Melissa's moans again. I can hear her breath ratcheting faster. I know she's working her fingers furiously in her panties. Gary whispers in my ear that he's watching Melissa touch herself and it's getting him harder. He moves faster in my mouth now, and I taste the first drops of his come.

Knowing that my best friend is watching my husband have his way with me drives me wild. Melissa's moans crescendo and I can tell she's about to climax. When Gary touches me again, I shudder deep inside. I can't scream or moan because I have Gary inside my mouth. Now Melissa begins to moan higher and higher, and I know she's coming. Gary works his finger expertly, and I can't control myself any longer. My moan is muffled as my body vibrates with powerful orgasm. My body is shaking the chair as spasm after spasm shoots through me.

I rest for a moment but Gary's movements in my mouth are quickening while at the same time his fingers are rubbing me faster and I can feel the tension building again. Then, without warning, another wave of satisfaction racks my body. With one final push, Gary comes. He sighs and moans as I swallow every last bit.

I hear Melissa's echoing footsteps as she leaves the room.

Janie Johnson

What a wonderful twist on the classic cherry-popping fantasy.

Virgin Territory

Henry drained his scotch, setting the glass on the coffee table. His hand shook slightly as he licked his lips nervously.

"Another one?" Bridget refilled his glass before he could answer.

"Thanks." Henry raised his glass. "Cheers."

Bridget shifted in her chair, sipping her scotch pensively. She watched as Henry picked a piece of lint from his neatly pressed pants. He was nervous, that was clear. *What on earth did he want?* The only time she'd spoken to him before was when he installed new software on her office computer. Certainly, he had never been to her home before. He was attractive, in a mildly geeky way. She guessed he was about thirty, a good fifteen years younger, but she was on the executive team and he was just some computer technician or whatever in the IT department, certainly not her area of expertise, and she'd never spoken to him other than telling him she would be gone for a meeting for about an hour while he installed the software and advising him to be careful of her hand-carved, walnut wood desk as it was her own personal piece of property and not something to be mistreated like a cubicle dweller's company-allocated faux-wood workspace. Bridget is not known for being soft. Perhaps that's why he was here. *Had he damaged her desk and she'd not noticed?* she thought. *Impossible.* Nothing escapes Bridget's notice.

"I might as well get right to it." Henry leaned back. "I need you to take my cherry."

"What!" Bridget almost dropped her glass.

"You don't think a man my age really wants to say that twice, do you?" Henry blushed.

Bridget leapt up. "Are you nuts?!"

Henry lunged for her, grabbing her wrist, causing her glass to spill scotch all down her blouse.

"I just thought, you being you, you might be willing." Henry smiled slyly.

"What?!"

"Your computer."

"What about my computer, you weasel?" Bridget glared at him. A lesser man would have slunk away, afraid for his testicles. Henry, it seems, was not a lesser man. "You read through my computer files?" Her face got hotter.

"Computers are funny things. You think you've erased information but it's still there, somewhere."

"You little fucker."

"Actually, that's the point. I'm not a fucker. . . . Oh relax. Your secrets are safe with me. Besides, I just confided my biggest secret to you. I trust you. You can trust me." Henry eased his grip on her wrist, smiling more pleasantly. "I can't wait to see you in 'costume.' "

"What's that supposed to mean?" Bridget knew it was useless pretending, but felt she had to try.

"The stuff you ordered online."

"You looked at my order." Bridget's tone was flat. It wasn't a question. She'd never felt so exposed, manipulated, and violated all at once. It was making her wet.

"I wanted to be sure you were the right woman for the job." Henry clumsily tried to touch her hair. "Teach me. Please."

Bridget looked into his clear green eyes. There was an urgency there, a hunger so raw it spoke to her. Her nipples rose under her starched office blouse, her breathing came more quickly.

"I'll change." Bridget broke her stare, stalking down the hall to her bedroom.

Henry ran his fingers through his hair, hardly daring to breathe. Was it possible? Would he actually know the feel of his cock thrusting into her soft, warm, wetness instead of only knowing the feel of his hand? He had spent months working up his nerve to corner Bridget Hornsby. He knew the only solution to his problem was an experienced woman.

"Come in here," Bridget commanded through the open bedroom door.

She was standing in the center of the candlelit room, her shaved pussy framed by leather chaps. He felt dizzy from the blood rushing to his balls. Her breasts, housed in leather straps, were full above her toned waist. Gone was the business hair, instead her hair hung down in a wild red mane, streaked with a wide strip of white, giving her a wild, exotic look.

"On your knees." Bridget stamped a stiletto heel on the floor.

Henry dropped, her pussy an inch from his face. He was trembling.

Bridget felt his halting hot breath warming her. She knew that she would have to manage him carefully. He was so close to coming already and she intended to get her own pleasure from this impromptu session.

"Remove your shirt." Henry fumbled with his buttons, struggling with shaking fingers. Bridget slapped him. Not hard, but hard enough to get his attention.

"When I tell you to do something, you do it. Am I making myself clear?" she hissed.

"Ab-Absolutely." He stuttered as he quickly peeled off his shirt. Bridget admired his muscular chest. This guy must work out between tweaking computers.

"Lick me."

Henry's tongue slapped against her, searching vainly.

"Spread my lips. Like this." Bridget pulled herself apart, tilting her hips slightly to provide better access.

"Lick from the bottom upward. More spit, damn you. Again. Better. Now, search for my clit. Good. That's it. Now suck," she commanded as he frantically sought to obey.

Henry latched on, sucking earnestly.

"Easy. *EASY*. Gentle."

He was too eager, too rough. She was overwhelmed. His lips latched on harder. Bridget fought for control as wetness flooded from her, soaking his chin.

"Lick the juices."

His mouth released her clit and again with his tongue he started at her taint and worked his way up, between her lips, pulling and sucking at her. She raked his back with her fingernails.

"Take off your pants."

Henry fumbled with his belt, still with his face between her legs.

"You may stop licking."

Henry ignored her and kept greedily going. He was getting too close to coming. Bridget could tell. She grabbed his hair, yanked his head back, and, again, slapped him across the face.

"Stop. Take off your pants."

"I'm going to come," Henry stammered.

"You will come when I say and not a moment before." She pulled harder, his hair still held in her iron grip. "Understood?"

He nodded. "May I stand?"

"Yes."

Henry staggered to his feet, slid down his pants, kicking them away. His thick, curved, cock swung out nine inches, the head shining with moisture.

"Lie on your back."

Henry lay across the bed.

Bridget stood over him admiring the view. She was shocked he was a virgin, with such a gift jutting proudly upward. She gently pulled off his socks.

Picking up a bottle of massage oil from the bedside table, she poured some into her palm before rubbing her hands together. She crawled onto the bed, straddling his thighs.

Henry's skin tingled as she rubbed her oiled hands up his body, his balls felt heavy, cock throbbing.

Bridget squeezed his nipples. He was sweating with the strain of not coming. His hands were clenched, his jaw locked, his eyes staring wildly. Placing an oiled finger behind his balls, she stroked his perineum, pressing firmly as she traced from his anal pucker to the base of his cock.

"Please, now. I'm going to lose it," he panted.

"You will not lose it."

She pinched his sac with her sharp nails, causing him to bite his lips in pain. His body gleamed with oil and his delicious virgin cock was purple, wet, and twitching powerfully. She wanted him now.

"You will wait," she commanded as she positioned herself above him. He could barely nod his agreement, but she knew what she was doing. She'd been doing this sort of thing, after all, for twenty-plus years. She placed his cockhead against her clit, stoking herself with it, moving it up and down.

"I can't hold on."

"Yes. You can." She dipped his head inside her and pulled it out.

Henry pounded his fists against the bed. "Please, please. I can't."

"You will." Bridget smacked a hand sharply across his face. She dipped him inside her again and pulled him out.

"Touch me. Touch my nipples. Grip them between your finger and thumb. Now, pull. Not so hard, you ass. There. Like that." Again, Bridget educated Henry on her pleasure.

She was ready. Clasping his shaft, she impaled herself.

Henry felt her hot, silky pussy slide over him. Holding her exposed ass cheeks, he thrust himself up. Her red mane swung wildly as he pounded into her. His breath caught in his throat.

"Not yet." Her eyes gleamed wickedly in the candlelight. Bridget leaned forward and latched onto his lips. She plunged her tongue deep into his mouth. She began to shudder, ready now. Hissing into his open lips, she gave him the command. "Come."

Henry thrust his massive cock into her. She pushed herself down to meet him. Her ecstasy mingled with his as they came together.

"Why the wait?" Bridget asked as she handed him his jacket at the door an hour later.

"I was afraid," he answered, after a pause.

"Afraid?"

"My dick." Henry rubbed his sweaty forehead.

"What about it?"

"It's crooked. You know." He flushed pink. "A girl laughed."

"Idiot."

"Maybe she was." Henry ran his fingers through her hair. "It was a long time ago."

"Not her. You. I'm going to have to smack some intelligence into you, starting Thursday next week at 6:45. Do not be late and . . ." She paused. "Bring me a new blouse to replace the one you ruined tonight."

Henry smiled. "Whatever you say, Bridget."

"That's 'Professor Hornsby' to you."

"Yes, Professor Hornsby."

Sasha Channing

JennaTip #11: Bent Penis

Yes, any shape, color, size of your body that works well is natural. However, sometimes a bent penis does not work, as in it is painful when erect, cannot grow erect causing impotence, causes pain to the partner, or any number of other problems. This sort of curvature may be caused by Peyronie's Disease. If you are suffering from these symptoms, please see a physician.

If, however, your penis has always curved or you have only a slight bend that is not increasing or you really think that the curvature is being caused by always wearing your cock to the left or genetics or whatever, *and* you have a good fulfilling sex life, then don't worry about it. Plenty of men have a slight bend or curve to their cock without any ill effects. It sometimes can even be a boon. Imagine if the curve goes just the right way then the cock just might tap the G-spot (or prostate if you're so inclined).

A bent penis can also be fun. If it curves upward, get some rings and play ring toss. Have it hold the towel while your partner showers if you've got the stamina and motivation.

No matter what, remember that in the end what matters more than a slight bend or curve is attention, skill, communication, and desire to please.

In Vegas there's a great bar at Caesar's where the girls dance behind screens, creating just the right silhouette. It's sexy as hell. Maybe I'll set one up in my bedroom.

Sienna

Dewy and pink from a long hot bath, Sienna stalked into her playroom. Eight feet of folding parchment screen divided the area in two. One half was equipped as a dressing room. In the other half was an oversized bed . . . and Paul. He was sitting on the edge, naked, his wrists manacled behind him. He'd been perched there for an hour now. It does a man good to be kept waiting, Sienna mused to herself, humming softly under her breath some dark, haunting melody she half remembered from years earlier from some dungeon she'd enjoyed.

Sienna adjusted the floor lamp to throw her shadow onto the screen, so that Paul could see her silhouette from the other side. She stretched, arms high, torso elongated, breasts lifted. Her shadow was so sharp that the conical peak of her nipple, crowning the lush curve of her breast, was clearly defined. She heard a muted gasp. Sienna didn't have to see to know that even if Paul's cock had softened while he waited, it was rigid now.

She caressed her body, cupping, squeezing, and jiggling her breasts on her palms. She was careful. Appearing relaxed, she was acutely aware of her angle to the light, needing to be certain that her silhouette showed exactly what she was doing as she took a nipple between finger and thumb and shook a resilient mound. She arched and undulated, smoothing her hands down her belly, stroking skin that was satin stretched over warm marble. Sienna bent at her hips, upper body horizontal, and shook her shoulders to sway her pendant breasts. A sharp intake of breath from the other side of the screen was her reward.

She turned her back to the light and spread her legs. Between the shadows of her slim thighs, an indented bow showed off how plump the cushion of her pussy was. Then, turning sideways, she leaned back and thrust her mound forward, hands on the backs of her thighs.

Paul's cock would be straining, thrusting from his thighs, foreskin retracted to expose the delicious plum of its head. Perhaps it was wet already. He'd be desperate, but Sienna planned to extend his torment until he was groaning incoherently. He was intelligent, suave, and sophisticated. Reducing such a man to a slavering mindless animal amused Sienna. If she were totally honest, it more than "amused" her. She might conceal her excitement, outwardly, but deep inside she was fizzing with pleasure.

Sitting at her dressing table, Sienna saw that Paul had laid everything out for her precisely as she liked. She'd trained him well.

She brushed her long black hair, elbows held high so that her jiggling breasts showed distinct shadows. After a full one hundred strokes, she gathered her locks on the very top of her head and pulled them through an ebony cone. The spray of her hair added four inches to her height before cascading down her back in a long ponytail.

Next came her face. Sienna started with foundations. She had been blessed with fine bone structure but she liked to emphasize the prominence of her cheekbones. Smears of a lighter shade above and dabs of rouge below her cheekbones gave her a feral look. Pale powder muted the effect.

Sienna used a pencil to outline her lashes, drawing each line beyond the corners of her eyes at an upward angle to make them look more tilted, more *wicked*. White lines, penciled between the black, made them more dramatic. She blended charcoal eye shadow with blue until her eyelids looked glossy and heavy.

Her lips were outlined in deep crimson. She filled them in with a slightly less intense shade and then coated them until they looked dripping wet.

Satisfied with her face, she dabbed an oversized powder puff into tinted body talc and stood up. Lifting her feet alternately onto her bench, she stroked powder from her toes, up over her sculpted ankles, along the smooth curves of her calves and up her thighs.

Paul sighed.

She pushed her bottom back to coat the roundness of its cheeks, then tugged them apart so that she could powder between them. She thrust her belly forward to trace its contours with a light dusting. Sienna slowed down when she reached her breasts. Each was lifted to be talcumed beneath. Each had its nipple brushed with delicate, slow strokes.

Paul made little mouth noises. Sienna knew that now his cock would *definitely* be drooling.

Sienna tossed her puff aside and considered her next move. Thong or boots, she pondered, finger to lips, hips tilted ever so slightly to the side. She decided on the thong, but first there was something else to do. Her delicate fingers dipped an oversized eyedropper into a bottle of strawberry oil. Standing with her legs spread, she parted her moist lips and slid the dropper up inside herself. Her fingers squeezed. Oil squirted. It was cold at first but soon warmed. She pinched her lips together to hold the pool of oil inside and stepped through the thin straps of her thong. Pulling it up, she allowed her lips to part a fraction as she fitted it snugly to her pussy. The thong was made of skin-thin black latex. It looked incredibly sexy but the best thing about it was the vertical ridge that fit between her lips and the small hard beads along the ridge's edge. She could feel each pea-sized globe, especially the one that nestled exactly where the head of her clitoris protruded from its sheath. She felt oil, blended with her own juices, trickle.

She sat so as to trap as much fluid as possible and then set about to put on her boots. They also were made of thin black latex, rolled down for now. The pencil-slim heels of her boots were a full six inches high, so that she had to point her feet like a ballerina to toe into them. Each boot's leg was slowly rolled up and smoothed to be wrinkle-free. They reached up her thighs to within three inches of her groin and indented her flesh where they gripped.

On those heels, and with her hair up, she was now taller than Paul would be, if she allowed him the privilege of standing erect, which wasn't likely.

Sienna wrapped her corset around her narrow waist. The corset, too, was black and made of latex, but thicker and heavily boned. Its top was shaped to rise between her breasts, with quarter cups that lifted her pink orbs. It came down exactly to her navel. She deftly hooked the front before she reached behind for the laces. With a thumb in each loop, she pulled hard to each side. Watching her silhouette, she saw her slender waist shrink by a full four inches. Deftly, she tied the laces securely. Tightly bound around her middle, she felt compressed and uncomfortably stiff. The way the cinching emphasized the jut of her breasts and the triumphant flare of her hips made it worthwhile.

Back rigidly straight, she sat again. Paul had laid out three collars for her. She selected the black leather one that was four inches wide and decorated with two-inch metal spikes. With it buckled in place, forcing her to hold her neck stretched and her head high, she applied the final touches. Dabbing a camel hair makeup brush into a pot of black liquid latex, she delicately and lovingly coated each nipple from the rim of its areola to its rounded tip. When she was satisfied with her art and the latex had dried, she applied a little latex polish and buffed each raven cone to a glossy shine.

Done!

All that was left was to choose which instrument to use on Paul. He'd set out a selection in a neat row. Sienna rejected the cane and the cat because they didn't match her outfit. The crops were fun but they didn't suit her mood. She felt energized, ready to apply a vigorous flogging, so she opted for the strap, fifteen inches of black leather on a six-inch ebony handle.

She strode from the screen's concealment. Paul gasped and trembled in a very satisfying way.

"Assume the position!" she commanded.

His cock jutting before him like the prow of a yacht, he scrambled to obey. Kneeling on the bed, face buried in its satin sheet, her victim raised his lean rump. Sienna paused for a moment to admire the way his heavy balls dangled in their sac between his thighs before lifting her sadistic toy.

"Are you ready?"

His muffled groan answered her.

"Then, dear husband, I think twenty this time."

His protest at the harsh promise was cut off by his yelp as the strap landed.

Morgana Baron

JennaTip #12: Take Time to Primp

L'Oreal had an ad campaign once upon a time that said their products were expensive, but "you" are worth it. *You are.* Spend some time primping, relaxing, and taking care of you. Eat good food that is healthy, take a long walk and enjoy the day, put oils in your bath, and listen to music you love. Buy a scent you love, spend a little extra on some good lingerie (for you or for your lover) get a massage, something . . . everything. Why not try primping and getting all powdered up as foreplay like in "Sienna" even if you don't conclude with a good, hard spanking.

You can also try putting some of that time and energy into taking care of your partner. Fill a bath with scented oils, light some candles, get out a nice scrubbing sponge, and bathe one another. Don't let ten years together and a couple of kids make you lazy about how you feel and appear. It's easy to give up but it's also pretty damn easy not to and so much more fun.

If you're in the mood for a little dress-up, get a set of cuffs,
mirror sunglasses, and a big, black, rough baton. I'll
let you decide how to use it all. I personally need to take
a little fifteen-minute break right about now just
thinking about it.

The Policewoman's Ball

He cruised right though it.

She was going to have to teach this person a little regard for the safety of others. She put on her siren and pulled out behind the vehicle.

The fact that it took the driver a few moments to finally pull the white VW bug over to the side of the road and the presence of a glinting surfboard on its roof made her suspect that she might even have a possible DUI on her hands. Profiling? Maybe. Who doesn't make snap judgments about people now and again? As an officer of the law she had been served well by such snap judgments more than once.

She put on her best officious law-enforcement face and approached the driver's side window. The driver poked his head out a bit and looked up submissively.

He definitely did not have the face of a hardened criminal. It was as smooth and open as the beach he was trying to reach. He was shirtless and wearing sandals. She knew his mind was on some tasty waves instead of the road.

"Do you know why I pulled you over?"

She could barely see his eyes beneath his bleached-out bangs, but she bet that he was mustering up a patented look of vacant confusion that had probably rescued him from many an unsavory situation in the past.

"Uh, no, Officer. Is there, like, a problem?"

"You ran a stop sign back there."

He flipped the hair off his face and pierced her with deep, bedroom eyes. "I thought I came to a complete stop, Officer. I'm real good about taking my time."

Okay, cute. But, there was still the matter of fulfilling responsibility.

"License and registration."

He winced, charm thwarted. He pulled his license and registration from the visor and handed them over. She peered at the smiling photograph and realized that it was pretty hot for a DMV snapshot. Twenty-two years old, barely an adult, but an adult nonetheless and a nicely chiseled one, too. If she had met him under different circumstances, she would be giving him her phone number instead of a citation.

As she reached for her pad, Surfer Boy decided to make a last-ditch attempt at charming away the impending fine. "C'mon, you don't want to write me up. I just want to go ride some waves. But, now that you're here, I can think of a few other things I'd like to ride."

Cheeky bastard. Cute, charming, sexy, cheeky bastard with a great smile and nice, white teeth looking up at her and licking his lips and making her think things she should not think.

"What makes you think I won't bust you for a 288?"

"Because whenever I look at you, I think '69.' Under those blues, I can tell you're red hot."

Most men never try to play the flirt card when confronted with a woman in a position of authority. The fact that he brazenly had done just that, throwing down the Jack of Hearts, so to speak, showed that he had balls. The fact that he could look beyond her uniform to take note of what incredible shape she was in showed that he had good taste. Still, he had to be taught a lesson.

"Step out of the vehicle."

He got out of the car and stood before her. For the first time, she could appraise him completely and she liked what she was seeing. He was tall, despite his relaxed posture, nicer pecs than she first realized, and had washboard, courtesy of surfboard, abs.

"Turn around, please."

He obeyed. Nice butt, even encased in baggy, loose trunks. She began to notice that her uniform felt especially tight, all of a sudden. It squeezed her chest and pulled at her crotch, making her body long for air.

Assuming the worst, the surfer placed his hands on his car, leaned over, and spread his legs. In a flash, she pictured herself in that very position. She blinked to clear her mind and approached him.

Since he assumed he was going to be frisked, she didn't want to disappoint him. She ran her hands down his sides and immediately realized how toned his body was. She then placed her hand between his legs. As her fingers brushed his inner thigh, all pretense of police ethics went out the window. She cupped him in her hand.

Satisfied, she handcuffed him. It was difficult, as her hands were trembling slightly.

She led him by the arm to her cruiser. Opening the door, she pushed his head down and guided him into the backseat. Then, casting a glance about her to make sure that there were no witnesses, she climbed in beside him.

She produced her keys and, as she uncuffed him, noticed the thick erection that tented his swim trunks obscenely. The little shit had gotten a hard-on on his arrest walk!

"Normally, I'd run you in and some judge would slap your ass with community service. I'm going to save myself a trip and some paperwork and sentence you myself." She also was considering slapping his ass.

A sly smile splashed across his face and he moved to speak.

She placed her hand over his mouth. "Honey, you have the right to remain silent."

Her other hand slipped down to the V of her slacks and she began to rub herself vigorously. She narrowed her eyes and instructed him, "You're going to service me, not the community. And if I don't climax, you're under arrest."

He looked like a kid in a candy shop. Was it just that standard temporary loss of rational thought that immediately preceded sex for men or did he really find her exceptionally hot?

She kept her holster on as she slipped out of her trousers. His hands were eagerly at her waistband. Enthusiastic, he threw her legs apart. Who did he think was in charge here? She secured a grip on his head and gave a good hard tug as she ran her fingers through his hair to clue him in.

Her foot slid along the partition separating the front and back seats as he went to work

He licked her like the sea breeze, at first, light and soft then more aggressively as though an afternoon storm were brewing. She began to forget about writing that ticket. This was the ticket. She rocked slowly back and forth and her little pink cadet stood at attention.

He felt her erect on his tongue, her tide coming in as he worked her. His mouth started to ride her harder now and his tongue dove even deeper.

He was working wonders on her. She braced herself on the seats and her wave came crashing thunderously in and she wailed like a siren as she came. She was trembling, useless, lost in a carnal daze.

Then, he took her by surprise. He rose on to his knees and swiftly pulled down his waistband. Those trunks, she thought at once, were baggier than she'd realized. He was enormous.

He cut off her ability to think when he slipped into her. She exhaled deeply, relaxing so she could take all of him.

She didn't think it was possible for her to come harder than she already had, but she didn't anticipate the rod he was packing. As he stretched her, her nerve endings went haywire again, causing her to moan.

As she came to her senses, she perceived a change in his breathing. She would have to act fast. She pushed him out roughly and sat up.

He blinked at her, disappointed. Desperate for his own payoff, he went to grasp himself but she halted him.

"I think we're done here."

"But, what about the serve part of 'To Protect and to Serve'?"

"Look, honey, you dodged the ticket. If I were you, I would hightail it while the getting's good."

He realized it was no use arguing. He smiled and shook his head, realizing that the policewoman's ball was over. He tucked himself back into his trunks and got out of the cruiser.

She watched him get back into his bug and take off for the sea and sand. He was careful to come to a complete stop at the next intersection. She had made a difference, she thought, putting someone on the straight and narrow. She loved wearing a badge and all the perks that came with it.

Robin Foreman

About Sounds Publishing, Inc.

Sounds Publishing, Inc. was founded in 2004 by the husband-and-wife team of Brian and Catherine OliverSmith with the goal of bringing high-quality romantic and erotic content to life in a variety of media. As the leading provider of romance and erotica in audio, one of the cornerstone principles of the company is to produce healthy, sexy erotica encouraging people to increase romance, intimacy, and passion through fantasy.

About the Editor

M. Catherine OliverSmith is the cofounder and editor-in-chief of Sounds Publishing, a co-venture with her spouse, Brian OliverSmith. She is the editor of hundreds of short stories and more than nine compilations and anthologies, served as editor-in-chief of *The Docket*, the official newspaper of the UCLA School of Law, and is the mother of two beautiful girls.

She would like to thank her husband, partner, lover, and best friend, Brian, for making good on his promise that life would never be boring.

About the Cover Photographer

Photographer Mike Ruiz is best known for his high-impact, colorful celebrity and fashion photography. His artistic objective is to present an upscale fashion edge to sensuality with aspirational images of iconic personas. Of all the celebrities he has photographed—from Kirsten Dunst to Ricky Martin to Christina Aguilera, just to name a few—he says he can count on one hand those that he believes truly possess the special unique magic to light up a camera. Jenna Jameson is one.

A mutual friend introduced Ruiz to Jameson for a spec shoot that turned out to be so successful, Jameson asked Ruiz to create the images for her new series of erotica, JennaTales. "Jenna has this amazing chemistry with the lens," explains Ruiz. "She loves the camera and the camera reciprocates that love. Every shot is beautiful."

Though a majority of his work has been with major magazines like *Vanity Fair* and *Interview* in the U.S., and European publications such as *Italian Elle*, *Arena*, and *Dazed and Confused*, Mike Ruiz has contributed to several books including Dolce and Gabbana's *Hollywood* and Iman's *The Beauty of Color*.

In addition to his editorial assignments, Ruiz has shot advertising campaigns for Sean John, MAC Cosmetics, and Reebok. He worked alongside rapper Lil Kim to create the image for her Royalty watch line and has recently branched out as a director, creating music videos for Traci Lords and Kelly Rowland.

This fall, Mike Ruiz made his feature film directorial debut with *Starrbooty*, a new madcap spy/comedy adventure starring the original supermodel of the world, RuPaul. For more information on Mike Ruiz and his projects, visit his website at www.mikeruiz.com.

PUT DOWN THE BOOK . . . and experience hot, sexy, erotica in a whole new hands-free way!

Sounds Publishing offers a wide variety of short audio erotica via download at www.jennatales.com and other online retailers. Visit www.jennatales.com for a FREE erotic tale from the Sounds Publishing collection today. Browse the several titles available for hands-free enjoyment on your MP3 player, iPod, burned to a CD, or directly on your computer.

Other titles from Sounds Publishing, Inc.

In print:

JennaTales: Erotica for the Woman on Top
Something Blue (January 2008)
Lip Service (July 2008)
Happy Endings (September 2008)
The Bottom Line (January 2009)

In audio:

Dulce Amore	*Tongue & Tied*
Melt Away	*A Lick & a Promise*
Kiss Your Ear	*Bend, Lick, Insert, Send*
Nibbles & Bites	*You've Got Tail*

Share Your Fantasies—Be a JennaTales Contributor!

Why not share your favorite, hottest, and best fantasy with the world? Send Sounds Publishing your short, erotic tale for **Jenna-Tales,** *Erotica for the woman on top* and if it is chosen to be included in a future **JennaTales** anthology or developed into an audio story, receive a free CD with your story or an autographed copy of the book in which it appears.

Visit www.jennatales.com for submission guidelines and official rules.

Ask Jenna About . . .

In developing **JennaTips,** *Sex tips for the woman on top,* we want to answer *your* burning questions. Tell us exactly what it is you want. Maybe one of the stories really lit your fire and you want more details about how to act it out. Maybe you're just curious about something you've heard about, read about, seen performed, or imagined.

Visit www.jennatales.com and click on the Ask Jenna! link to e-mail us your question. Keep your eye out for the upcoming **JennaTips,** *Sex tips for the woman on top* books.

Become the woman on top.